"You need a new wife, and I've decided maybe God picked out Ms. Ellie to be her."

Kristie clasped her hands together. "Remember the Bible story yesterday about how God picked out Rebecca for Isaac, to be his wife? Well, I was helping God's plan by letting you be together without me. So maybe you'd kiss Ms. Ellie."

Ellie couldn't look at Quinn—not until the memory faded of that moment in the meadow when she'd thought he was going to kiss her.

"Kristie, none of us knows what God intends," she finally said.

Kristie grabbed her hand. "But don't you like my daddy, Ms. Ellie?"

She willed her voice to be steady. "Of course I do. But that doesn't mean I'd be the right wife for him. That's something you have to let your daddy decide." But in spite of her words, she prayed Quinn would. Because she'd begun to fall in love with him.

Books by Marta Perry

Love Inspired

A Father's Promise #41
Since You've Been Gone #75
*Desperately Seeking Daddy #91
*The Doctor Next Door #104
*Father Most Blessed #128
A Father's Place #153

*Hometown Heroes

MARTA PERRY

began writing children's stories for Sunday school take-home papers while she was a church educational director. From that beginning she branched into writing magazine fiction and then book-length fiction. She's grateful for the opportunity to write the kind of books she loves to read.

Marta lives in rural Pennsylvania with her husband of thirty-seven years, and they enjoy visiting their three grown children scattered around the globe. In addition to writing and travel, Marta loves hearing from readers and enjoys responding to their letters. She can be reached c/o Steeple Hill Books, 300 East 42nd Street, New York, NY 10017.

A Father's Place
Marta Perry

♥ *Love Inspired*®

Published by Steeple Hill Books™

STEEPLE HILL BOOKS

Steeple
Hill™

ISBN 0-373-87160-0

A FATHER'S PLACE

Copyright © 2001 by Martha P. Johnson

Visit us at www.steeplehill.com

Printed in U.S.A.

Many waters cannot quench love;
rivers cannot wash it away.
—*Song of Songs* 8:7

This story is dedicated with love and gratitude
to my friends in Christ at First Church.
And, as always, to Brian.

Prologue

Prayers from Bedford Creek, Pennsylvania

Father, please remember my son, Quinn. He's so bitter now, and if only he'd come home, maybe I could help him....
Please, Lord, bless my brother, Quinn, and help him to see that he has to forgive....
And God bless my daddy, and bring him back home to stay. Please don't forget that I'd like a new mommy, and if it's okay with You, I think my Sunday school teacher, Ms. Ellie, would be just perfect....

Chapter One

He'd come home to the town where he no longer belonged, to break up his mother's romance. Put like that, Quinn Forrester decided it didn't sound like a creditable goal. It wouldn't impress the woman he was about to see, and he needed Ellie Wayne's cooperation. Either that, or he needed her surrender.

The tension that had driven him for days cranked up a notch. His natural instinct was to explode, demanding explanations, but that wouldn't work. He'd have to exercise diplomacy to get what he wanted from Ellie Wayne, and his talent for that had grown rusty over years of fighting nature's rampages in places considerably wilder than this one.

He glanced along the narrow street. Bedford

Creek, Pennsylvania, spread up a narrow cleft in the mountains from the river. Its frame houses climbed the hillside in steps, as if they'd been planted there.

Ellie Wayne's craft shop was on the lowest street, along with the police station, a few other small shops and a scattering of houses. Opposite it, the park spread along the flood-prone land by the river. His practiced engineer's eye automatically noted the water level, higher now from the frequent rain than was usual for August.

The craft shop, the lower floor of a frame house, had been a newsstand when he was a boy, when Bedford Creek was a sleepy backwater where nothing ever happened. Then some energetic citizens had decided to capitalize on turn-of-the-century architecture and wooded mountain scenery.

Since then, like much of the town, the shop had been transformed into a quaint attraction for the tourists who deluged the village during the summer and fall. He stepped around a man with a camera, dodged two women laden with shopping bags and stopped.

Ellie Wayne had an eye for display—he'd give her that. An artfully draped quilt brightened the shop window, surrounded by handwoven baskets and dried-flower wreaths in colors that picked up the quilt's faded earth tones. A yellow stuffed cat snuggled into a needlework cushion.

He'd planned his visit for closing time on this busy summer Saturday, hoping to catch her alone after the last of the shoppers left. He didn't want any eavesdroppers on the conversation he was about to have.

He took a breath, tried to curb his impatience and reached for the door. A bell jangled, and the cool, dim interior invited him in. The woman behind the worn oak counter glanced up, her brown eyes registering his presence. But she wasn't alone yet. Two last-minute customers fingered a quilt that was spread across the counter, peppering her with questions.

He moved behind a display table heaped with woven tablecloths and inhaled the faint, spicy aroma of dried flowers. Every inch of the tiny shop displayed something—his first impression was clutter; his second, coziness.

He intercepted a questioning glance from Ellie Wayne and pretended interest in a stack of hand-made baskets, tamping down his irritation.

"I'll be with you in just a moment." Her voice was as welcoming as the shop.

"No hurry." He forced cordiality into his tone. "I can wait." He could wait. When he talked to her, he wanted the woman's undivided attention.

Undivided attention—that was also what his mother and his six-year-old daughter wanted from him. They'd been reluctant to let him out of their sight since he arrived home yesterday, as if fearing he'd disappear back to the Corps of Engineers project that had occupied him for so long.

Too long, he realized now, far too long. It had been too tempting to bury himself in work after Julie's death, too easy to convince himself that Kristie was better off living with his mother in this comforting, safe place where nothing ever changed.

He gripped the oblong basket he'd picked up. Things had changed, and if he'd been a better father, a better son, he'd have realized that. Bedford Creek wasn't a safe little backwater any longer. The tourism boom had brought strangers to town—strangers like Ellie Wayne and her father.

He glanced toward the woman. Maybe it wasn't entirely fair to describe her as a stranger. She'd opened her shop four or five years ago, and he must have seen her playing the organ in church on his few visits home. But it was only in the last few months that Kristie had begun talking about Ms. Ellie so much, and even more recently that her innocent chatter had paired Grandma with Charles Wayne. And then his sister Rebecca had called, concerned about their mother's infatuation for a man she'd just met, and he'd known it was time to come home.

The customer produced a credit card. Apparently the transaction had been successful. Ellie smiled as she folded the quilt, her hands lingering as if she hated to part with it. A neat salesperson's gimmick, he decided. She probably hoped to sell them something else.

He assessed the woman, trying to look at her without preconceptions. Slim, tall, probably about thirty or so. A wealth of dark brown hair escaped from a woven headband to curl around her face. There was nothing conventional about Ellie's looks. Her face was too strong, her coloring too vivid, with those dark expressive eyes and the natural bloom in her cheeks.

Nothing conventional about her clothing choices, either. Today she wore a long skirt and an embroidered blouse that would look more at home in an artists' colony than in Bedford Creek. He shouldn't let that quick impression prejudice him against her, but he couldn't deny the feeling. She looked as if she didn't belong here.

The bell jangled as the customers went out, and he tensed. Ellie Wayne was an unknown quantity as far as he was concerned. He didn't want to do battle with her, but he would if he had to.

She came toward him with the quick, light step

of a dancer. "I'm sorry I kept you waiting. May I help you with something? I have those with different colors of reed woven in."

He glanced down at the basket he'd nearly forgotten was in his hands. "I'm not shopping."

Her eyes widened as if he'd insulted her wares, and he reminded himself he'd intended to be diplomatic. "It's very nice," he added, putting it down.

Faint wariness showed in those expressive dark eyes. Maybe it was her eyes, maybe it was the ethnic flavor of her clothing, but a thread of song wound through his thoughts, its lyrics warm and yearning, something about a brown-eyed girl. He shoved the distraction away.

"Then what can I do for you?" she asked.

"I'm here about my mother." She still looked at him blankly, of course. She didn't know him from Adam. "I'm Quinn Forrester. Gwen's son."

"Quinn?" Her voice lilted with surprise. If he expected guilt, he didn't get it. "Gwen didn't tell me you were coming home."

It was almost as if she should have been informed, and irritation flickered through him. "Does she tell you everything?"

"I didn't mean that." Warm color rose in her cheeks. "I'm just surprised she didn't mention it."

"Especially since you see so much of each

other.'' He didn't intend the words to sound accusing, but they did.

She stiffened, apparently sensing his attitude. ''Your mother and I are cochairing a craft show next month for the church.'' She said it carefully, as if weighing each word. ''So we have been seeing a lot of each other lately.''

''It's a little more than that, isn't it?'' He wasn't going to dance around the subject any longer. It was time the woman leveled with him. ''The way I hear it, your father's the one who's spending a lot of time with her.''

He couldn't be mistaken about her reaction to that—a flash of fear. She masked it, but not quickly enough.

Determination hardened inside Quinn. His father would have expected Quinn to protect his mother, not to bury himself in his own grief. But he hadn't, and now it looked as if Gwen Forrester, with her naive belief in people and her tempting little nest egg, was falling prey to a charming drifter who had no visible means of support and a murky background. Well, not if he could prevent it.

''I don't know what you mean.'' Her sudden pallor gave the lie to the words.

He shook his head. ''I think you do. I want to know what's going on between my mother and your father.''

* * *

The unexpected introduction of her father into the conversation sent Ellie's heart racing. What had Charles Wayne done now? Familiar panic flooded her. She'd known it spelled trouble when he showed up at her door after all these years. She should have told him to go away. She should have…

She took a grip on her frightened thoughts. This was ridiculous. She was overreacting. Something about Quinn Forrester's uncompromising expression had panicked her unnecessarily.

"I don't understand." She could only hope it came out calmly enough—that he hadn't seen that moment of fear.

Quinn leaned against the display table with what was probably meant to be a casual air. It didn't succeed. Nothing about his intensity was casual.

"It's not that difficult a question." He concentrated on her face as if he'd look right past her expression and into her mind. "What's going on between my mother and your father?"

"Going on?" She stared at him blankly. "Nothing. I mean, they hardly know each other. Why would you think something was going on?"

He moved toward her, bracing his hand against the worn wooden counter. He was too close, invading her space. She forced herself not to step back, knowing instinctively he'd interpret that as a sign of weakness.

"From what I've heard..." he began, when a yellow blur soared to the countertop next to him. Quinn snatched his hand back with a startled exclamation.

"Sorry." She took a steadying breath, trying to calm her stampeding pulse. "That's Hannibal. You're encroaching on his favorite place."

As this man was with her. This was her shop, she reminded herself. Her town, her place in the world. She belonged here now. She stroked the tomcat. Hannibal pushed his head firmly against her hand and then sat, folding front paws majestically under his white bib.

"I saw him in the window. I thought he was a stuffed toy." Quinn held out his hand. Hannibal sniffed cautiously, then deigned to let himself be scratched behind the ear.

She took another deep breath. *Calm down. Don't overreact.* Whatever Quinn wanted, it didn't necessarily have to be bad. She watched as he stroked the cat, giving it the same concentration he had her.

Quinn's daughter must have gotten her red hair and freckles from some other part of the family tree. His hair was a dark, rich shade of brown, the color of ripe chestnuts. Straight dark brows contrasted with surprisingly light eyes—not quite blue, closer to slate. His tanned skin and the feathering of sun lines around his eyes suggested years of outdoor work in a place far from this green Pennsylvania valley. He had a firm mouth and an even firmer chin that argued an uncompromising disposition.

He switched his gaze from the cat to her, and a little quiver of awareness touched her. That intent gaze was unnerving. It was much the same as the gaze with which Hannibal watched a bird before he pounced.

"As I was saying, about my mother and your father."

"Gwen is my friend." She hurried into speech, hoping to deflect whatever accusation was coming. "And my father is here for a visit. A brief visit," she added. "Naturally they've met each other."

"Because you and my mother are friends." His tone made it sound sinister.

She held her gaze steady with an effort. "Yes."

"It's a little more than that, I think." His concentration pinned her to the spot. "Each time I talk to Kristie on the phone, his name comes up. 'Charles and Grandma did this. Charles and Grandma did that.' He seems to have become almost part of the family in the last few weeks."

Her mind raced. When had all this been going on? She'd been busy, of course, but she should have known what her father was doing. Maybe she'd just felt relieved he'd found something to occupy himself in Bedford Creek. That way she didn't have to see him and constantly be reminded of the painful past.

"As I said, Gwen and I are working on the fundraiser together." She hoped her smile looked more convincing than it felt. "My father has been helping out, so I suppose he and Gwen have spent some time together."

"Some time?"

His persistence sparked the anger that had been hidden beneath her fear. "This is beginning to sound like an inquisition."

He didn't bother to deny it. "I have a right to worry about my family's welfare."

Meaning he thought she and her father threatened it. She stiffened, meeting his eyes with as much defiance as she could muster. "Your family isn't in danger from us."

"When my sixty-five-year-old mother starts acting like a schoolgirl with a new boyfriend, I worry. Try hard. Maybe you'll understand."

The temper she'd fought to control escaped. "I can't imagine when you had the chance to observe your mother. You've hardly been back in Bedford Creek in the past few years."

His fists clenched, and she saw in an instant she'd gone too far. She knew about the death of his wife, of course. She'd barely become acquainted with Julie when the woman's death in a car accident had shocked the whole town. In the two years or so since, according to Gwen, Quinn had buried himself in his work, as if to find escape. Now she'd challenged that.

"I'm sorry," she said quickly, before the situation could deteriorate any further. "I didn't mean that. And I certainly didn't have the right to say it."

"My work has kept me away." He said it calmly enough, but a muscle quivered in his jaw with the effort. "That doesn't mean I don't care."

She seemed to be juggling dynamite. "I'm sure you do. But Gwen..." She hesitated on the verge of pointing out the obvious—that Gwen was a grown woman who could manage her own life.

His gaze hardened, and she suspected he knew what she'd been about to say. "My mother's led a sheltered life. My father always protected her from any unpleasantness."

A spasm of memory clutched her. She'd led a fairly sheltered life, too, once upon a time, until her father's betrayal had blown it into a million pieces. If Charles really was somehow involved with Gwen, it was probably the worst idea he'd had since that disaster.

She wouldn't believe it. Quinn was probably

overreacting, but she knew instinctively he'd be a bad enemy to make. She couldn't afford to antagonize him any more than she already had.

"My father is just here for a brief visit. He regards Gwen as nothing more than a casual acquaintance." She hoped.

His frown was uncompromising. "If there's anything more—"

The jingling of the bell cut off what sounded like a threat. Ellie turned toward the door, and her heart sank. Why on earth had her father chosen this particular moment to come into the shop?

She glanced cautiously back at Quinn, and tension zigzagged like lightning along her nerves. He looked like a predator about to strike.

Quinn looked from Ellie's suddenly guilty face to the man who'd just entered. So this was the father—it had to be. Why else would she look that way? He'd almost been swayed by her protestations, but now all his suspicions flooded back.

"Sorry, my dear. I didn't realize you were busy with a customer." Charles Wayne stood, hand on the doorknob, his expression mingling regret at interrupting with curiosity.

"I'm just closing," Ellie said. "Maybe you could set the table for supper."

She gestured toward the stairs at the rear of the

shop, which must lead to the living quarters upstairs. Her desire to get her father out of his range was as clear as if she wore a sign announcing it.

He didn't intend to let that happen, not until he'd had a chance to see the man for himself. He took a step forward, holding out his hand. "You must be Ellie's father. I'm Quinn Forrester."

"Charles Wayne. What a pleasure to meet you. You're Gwen's son, of course. She talks about you all the time."

His smile was smoother than his daughter's, more practiced. He had to be in his sixties, but he had a quick, light step that made him look younger, as did the sparkle in his bright blue eyes.

"Gwen mentioned you were home when I ran into her and little Kristie at the grocer's," he went on. "A delightful child, isn't she?"

It was the trick of either a good salesman or a confidence man—to ask a question that would bring an affirmative answer. "I think so, but then I'm prejudiced."

And prejudiced against the man in front of him, he realized. Maybe it was the ready smile, or the glib chatter, but Charles Wayne put his back up. He preferred the daughter's quick antagonism to the father's charm.

"Dad." Ellie nodded toward the stairs. "I have soup in the slow cooker for our supper."

"Then we can have it anytime," Wayne said, apparently oblivious to her desire to get rid of him. He smiled at Quinn. "I believe Gwen told me you're working out west someplace."

"Oregon. I'm with the Corps of Engineers." He'd like to tell the man his profession was none of his business, but that wasn't the way to find out about more about him. He'd already come within a hair of outright war with the daughter. Maybe it was time to take a step back. His mother wouldn't be inclined to listen to his concerns if he started by alienating her friends. "Are you familiar with the West Coast?"

"Been there, of course. Now, this little town where my daughter's settled is a far cry from our old stamping grounds."

The tension emanating from Ellie jerked upward, evidenced by the indrawn breath, the tightening of her hands. So, there was something about that mention of where they were from that bothered her.

"And where was that?" he asked. "I don't think I've heard much about Ellie's past."

"I don't find people all that interested in my history." Ellie's casual tone wasn't very convincing.

"Odd, isn't it? People's stories are endlessly fascinating to me," Charles said. "There was a man I met when I was working in San Francisco, or was it Santa Fe? Doesn't matter. In any event, this man had actually taken part in a Mount Everest climb. Think of that.''

Quinn didn't intend to be distracted by mythical mountain climbers. ''You were saying you'd lived where?''

Charles gave an airy wave. ''All over the place. I'm afraid I'm the original tumbleweed. Just haven't been able to settle down in one place, unlike my daughter.'' He smiled fondly at Ellie, who looked strained. ''Ellen has certainly put down roots here in Bedford Creek. Not that it isn't a charming place, but it's not the life I expected her to have.''

''People have to make their own decisions about things like that.'' Ellie took his arm firmly and turned him toward the stairs. ''I'll be up soon, Dad. How about checking the soup for me?''

''Of course, of course.'' Charles glanced over his shoulder at Quinn. ''I'll look forward to seeing you again. We must talk longer the next time.''

If Ellie ever wanted to embark on a life of crime, Quinn decided, she'd have to do something about that expressive face. It showed only too clearly her relief at having gotten rid of her gregarious father and her conviction that he and Quinn wouldn't be having any more little talks.

Ellie glanced pointedly toward the exit. ''I should be closing now.''

I'm not as easy to be rid of as all that, he assured her silently. "Your father's quite the charmer, isn't he? I can see how my mother might find him entertaining company."

He had a sudden longing for his own father's solid, quiet presence. No one would have used charming or entertaining to describe John Forrester, but he'd been a man of strength and integrity.

"My father's charming to everyone." She smiled tightly. "It's his way. I don't think you need to worry that Gwen is susceptible to it. She's got a level head on her shoulders."

"You think so? I love my mother dearly, but levelheaded is the last thing I'd say about her. My father was always the dependable one in the family."

She lifted her eyebrows, as if doubting his assessment. "And now Rebecca is, I suppose."

Guilt stabbed at him. Since his father's death Rebecca had taken on the duty that should have been his. Their other sister, Angela, had married, then gone off to Philadelphia when her husband's business sent him there. And Quinn had been so preoccupied with the twin burdens of his career and his grief that he'd let Rebecca handle everything.

Not anymore, he promised, not sure whether he was talking to himself or his father. It was time he took on the responsibilities he'd shelved for too long.

"Rebecca has enough to do with her husband, the clinic and a baby on the way. If my mother needs anything, I'll be the one to help her."

He wasn't sure whether anger or fear predominated in the look she gave him. "I'm sure she appreciates that," she said. "Now if you'll excuse me, I have a meal to get ready."

He clearly wasn't going to get anything more from Ellie at this point, so he let himself be ushered to the door. Her relief was almost palpable when he finally set foot outside.

He stopped, hand on the door to keep her from closing it. "Where was it your father said the two of you were from?"

"Ohio," she snapped, and closed the door so sharply he had to snatch his hand away.

Ellie wasn't the accomplished storyteller he suspected her father was. That had had the ring of truth about it.

He watched as she flipped the Closed sign into place. She went toward the stairs, so quickly she might almost have been running away. The yellow cat leaped into the window, stared unblinkingly at him for a long moment and then turned and followed his mistress.

If he'd gone to Ellie Wayne's shop seeking assurance that everything was all right, he'd come away knowing the opposite was true. And it wasn't his adverse reaction to Charles Wayne that had convinced him. He could chalk that up to personal taste.

No, he'd been convinced by Ellie's reactions. Ellie Wayne was afraid. Of him? Of something to do with her father? He wasn't sure, just as he wasn't sure of a lot of things about her.

She'd lived in Bedford Creek for close to five years. She'd become an accepted part of the town. But as far as he could tell, no one knew much about her life before she came here. And people knew even less about her father.

It was time that changed, and he intended to change it.

Chapter Two

"**M**s. Ellie, do you really think God answers prayers?"

Ellie decided she'd never get used to small children's ways of asking the deepest spiritual questions. She sat down next to Quinn's little daughter the next morning. The rest of her Sunday school class had scampered out the door already, but Kristie had lingered, the question obviously on her mind.

"Yes, I think God does answer prayers." She brushed a coppery curl back from Kristie's cheek, sending up a silent plea for guidance. "But I think sometimes we don't understand God's answers."

Kristie frowned, putting both hands on the low wooden table. "I don't know what you mean."

"Why don't you tell me about your prayer," she suggested. "Maybe I can help you understand."

Kristie's rosebud mouth pursed in an unconscious imitation of her grandmother's considering look. "Well, see, I prayed just like you taught us. And I remembered to thank God and everything."

Their last few lessons had been on prayer. Kristie, at least, had been listening. "And what else?" she prompted gently.

"I asked God to make Daddy stay here for good." The words burst out. "And I thought it would work. But when I asked him, Daddy said he has to go out West again. And I don't want him to!"

Ellie drew the child close, heart hurting. Did Quinn realize how much his little girl missed him, even though a loving family surrounded her?

"Kristie, I know I said God answers our prayers, and I believe that." She spoke slowly. Caring for the spiritual well-being of the children in her class was one of the most important things she'd ever do, and she wanted to do it right.

"But God knows what's best for us. Sometimes the answer is yes, and sometimes it's no. And sometimes the answer is wait." She smiled into the little face turned up to hers so trustingly. "I think that's the hardest answer of all, because I hate to wait for things. But I remind myself that God loves me and wants what's best for me. Do you think you could remember that, too?"

"I guess so."

"I'm sure she will."

The unexpected masculine voice jolted her. Quinn stood in the doorway, and he'd obviously been listening for some time. Her cheeks flushed. Had he heard what Kristie's prayer was about? And was he angry that she presumed to give his daughter advice?

"Daddy!" Kristie raced across the room to throw her arms around his waist. "Are you going to church with me?"

"Sure thing, sweetheart." He gave her a quick hug, his face softening as he looked down at her.

Ellie's heart cramped. When he smiled at his daughter, the lines in Quinn's face disappeared. The marks of grief and bitterness were magically erased, and he looked again like the college graduate in the picture on Gwen's piano, smiling at the world as if he owned it.

"You run down to the parlor and catch up with Grandma, okay? I want to talk to your teacher for a minute."

Kristie nodded, the clouds gone from her face, and danced toward the door. "We'll wait for you," she said importantly. "Don't be late."

Yesterday it had been his mother; today it was his daughter. Quinn Forrester must feel she'd interfered with his family far too much.

Quickly, before he could launch an attack, Ellie shoved the Sunday school books onto the shelf. "I'm afraid I don't have time now." She started for the door. "I'm playing the organ for the service, and I have to get ready."

But if she thought she was going to get rid of him that easily, apparently she was mistaken. He fell into step beside her. A dark suit, pale blue shirt and striped tie had replaced yesterday's jeans, but he still looked like a man who belonged outdoors. And he moved as if the church hallway were a mountain trail.

"I'll walk with you, and we can talk on the way." He pushed open the double doors that led from the Sunday school wing to the church itself, his hand strong and tanned against the pale wood.

Maybe it was time to go on the offensive with him. "I suppose you think I shouldn't have spoken that way to your daughter." She certainly wouldn't apologize for doing what a church school teacher should.

Instead of counterattacking, Quinn tilted his head slightly as if considering. "No, I wouldn't say I think that. You're her Sunday school teacher. That's your job, answering the tough questions."

His unexpected agreement took the wind out of her sails, and she glanced up to meet his steady gaze. For now, at least, it wasn't accusing. "The questions are tough. Sometimes almost unanswerable.''

''What do you do if you don't have an answer?'' He really seemed curious.

She smiled. ''Say so. Then I ask the pastor. That's his job, after all.''

''I'm sure he appreciates that.''

She'd never have thought, after yesterday, that she and Quinn would be smiling at each other in perfect harmony. The tension inside her eased. They'd gotten off to a difficult start, but perhaps they could begin again. She didn't want to be on uncomfortable terms with Gwen's son.

They reached the vestry before she could think of anything else to say. Was that all Quinn wanted to talk with her about?

She reached into the closet and took out the shoes she wore for playing the pipe organ. She held them for a moment, waiting for him to speak, wondering if she should say anything more about Kristie.

When the silence stretched out, she looked up at him. ''I guess you overheard what Kristie's prayer was about.''

He nodded, a muscle flickering near his mouth, but he didn't say anything.

She took a deep breath. This was definitely not her business, but she couldn't ignore Kristie's prayers. "I don't know much about your job, but I know she'd love it if you could work closer."

Quinn's expression closed to a stiff, impenetrable mask. "That's not possible. I go where the Corps of Engineers sends me. Unlike your father, I'm not a gentleman of leisure."

Her stomach clenched. There was the counterattack she'd expected. "My father is retired." She forced the words out through suddenly stiff lips.

Quinn leaned toward her, making her aware of how tiny the vestry was. He was much too close, and he took up all the available space. "What is he retired from?"

She turned away, slipping on her shoes, buying time. So the battle wasn't over between them. His brief friendliness had evaporated, and he wanted answers she had no intention of giving him.

A tremor of fear shivered through her. If anyone in Bedford Creek knew the truth about her father, everyone would know. And if they did, the love and acceptance she'd grown to count on would vanish in an instant. She'd be alone again.

She straightened slowly and looked at Quinn. If she were a better liar, she might be able to throw him off the track, but she suspected that was impossible. "Business," she said crisply.

She hurried through the door to the organ loft, knowing she was running away from him, knowing, too, that it was futile. Quinn Forrester wasn't the kind of man to give up easily. He wanted the truth, but if he got it, he could destroy her happiness.

Quinn stood frowning after her for a moment. He'd like to pursue her and drag some answers out of her, but he couldn't. The opening notes already echoed from Grace Church's elderly pipe organ. Where had Ellie trained? That was yet another thing he didn't know about her.

He walked back through the hallway to the parlor. It was surprising how little the people in Bedford Creek seemed to know about Ellie Wayne. Even his mother, who was usually a clearinghouse of local information, only seemed to know tidbits: that she'd worked in a craft shop in Philadelphia; that her mother died when she was young; that she was an only child. Hardly the kind of information Bedford Creek usually amassed about newcomers.

And as far as Charles Wayne was concerned, the slate was even blanker, if possible. That was what had upset his sister enough to make her call him. No one knew anything, according to Rebecca, except that he was Ellie's father. He'd never visited her before; no one had ever heard her speak of him; he'd arrived by bus and didn't seem to have a car. A man whose background was that vague must have something to hide.

Quinn entered the parlor, trying to push his concern to the back of his mind. At least Gwen would be safely separated from Charles Wayne for the next hour. After church, like it or not, he'd have the private talk with her that she'd managed to avoid for the last two days.

His mother and Kristie waited with Rebecca and her husband. He put his arm around Rebecca, kissing her cheek.

"How's my little sister?" He looked at her closely. "Kind of washed-out these days, aren't you?" He sent a mock glare in Brett's direction. "Have you been working her too hard at the clinic?" He knew Rebecca loved her work as a physician's assistant at the town clinic, especially since her husband was the doctor she assisted. Together they took care of the whole town.

Brett Elliot grinned, holding up both hands in surrender. "Not me, I promise. Blame your new little niece or nephew."

"Speaking of which..." Rebecca's face seemed tinged with green. She shook her head and rushed off in the direction of the rest room.

"What's wrong with Aunt Rebecca?" Kristie pulled at Brett's sleeve. "Is she sick?"

"Sometimes ladies have upset tummies when they're going to have a baby," Brett said easily while Quinn was still considering how to answer that question. Thank goodness for a doctor in the family. "I'll see if she feels like staying or wants to go home. Catch you later."

The choir passed them, heading into the choir loft, and Kristie grabbed his hand. "Come on, Daddy. I want to get a story paper before they're all gone."

He let himself be drawn toward the sanctuary and followed his mother and daughter into the pew, automatically tensing. He glanced at his mother. Did she have the same thoughts he did each time he entered this space?

Kaleidoscopic images flowed into each other—standing at the communion table for his confirmation, holding Julie's hand while they said their vows, watching his sisters get married. Unfortunately the happy images were swamped by the sad ones of sitting in the front pew looking bleakly at his father's coffin and then, too soon, at Julie's. He swallowed hard, trying to get rid of the knot in his throat, and concentrated on the arrangements of roses on either side of the chancel.

A flutter of movement at the end of the pew distracted him, and he watched with disbelief as his mother half stood to wave to Charles Wayne. In another moment she'd beckoned the man to join them, and Wayne was sliding into the pew next to her as if it were the most natural thing in the world.

The organ sounded the notes of the opening hymn, and he stood, seething silently. So much for his assumptions about the way this morning would go. He sent his mother a look that he hoped conveyed his feelings, and she smiled back blandly, as if she enjoyed disconcerting him.

He tried to concentrate on the service, tried not to be distracted by Charles's presence in the family pew or by memories of the past. It wasn't easy.

Kristie pinched his arm, and he leaned over for her soft whisper. "Ms. Ellie plays pretty, doesn't she?"

He nodded. The organ was half-hidden by the pulpit, but he could see Ellie when she leaned forward. Her dark hair curled around her face as her hands moved to the organ stops. Her expression unexpectedly touched him. She was transported; that was all he could think.

His gaze lingered on the line of her cheek, the soft smile that curved her lips. If not for the problem posed by her father, he might be thinking how attractive she was. Not his type, but appealing, with her vivid coloring and quick grace.

In an instant he rejected the thought, appalled at himself. The pain of Julie's death at the hands of a drunk driver was with him every day, even after two years. On the job, preoccupied with work, he managed to hold it at bay.

But here in Bedford Creek, where they'd married, where she'd chosen to live when the corps sent him out West, it wasn't possible. Each time he came home he had to mount a guard against the sudden onslaught of memory, pain, anger.

He'd thought the anger would go away once the driver was in prison where he belonged, but that hadn't happened. Instead it had stayed, burning at the back of his mind, singeing his very soul.

He forced himself to pay attention to the message. *Just concentrate, and the service will soon be over.* He'd take his mother and daughter home, then sit his mother down for a serious talk about the danger to a well-off, naive widow posed by glib strangers.

The last Amen sounded, and he tried to hustle his little party toward the door. But at least half the congregation wanted to greet him, and he couldn't be rude, even though the sight of Charles lingering at his mother's side sent his blood pressure rising.

With a sense of relief he saw Ellie heading toward them, shedding her robe as she came. She'd probably detach her father.

"Ellie, dear, that was lovely." His mother hugged her, then turned to him. "Wasn't it lovely, Quinn?"

He felt about eight years old, being prompted by

his mother to say the right thing. "Beautiful. You play very well. Where did you study?"

"Here and there." She caught her father's arm, tugging it a bit. "Come on, Dad, time to go home."

"But you're not going home," his mother exclaimed. "I've already talked to Charles, and it's all settled. You and your father are coming to Sunday dinner with us."

To do her justice, Ellie looked just about as appalled at that suggestion as he must. "That's very nice of you, Gwen, but I'm afraid we have to get home."

"Nonsense," his mother said briskly, linking her arm with Ellie's. "I know you haven't started dinner yet, and I have a pot roast cooking that's just about ready. We insist you come, don't we, Quinn?"

In other circumstances, this would be comic. Ellie clearly didn't want to come, any more than he wanted her to. Just as clearly, they were both stuck.

"Please join us," he said.

Ellie shot him one wary look, and then she nodded. Like it or not, the Forresters and the Waynes were having Sunday dinner together. Maybe this was his chance to get closer to her. He frowned. That should not be making him feel anticipation.

"Dad, please. Before we get there, you have to tell me about you and Gwen." Ellie turned onto the street where the Forresters lived, her stomach tightening. They'd be there in moments, and she still hadn't gotten a satisfactory answer from her father.

She felt him studying her face and kept her eyes on the road. "Princess, I…"

"Don't call me that!" The nickname took her relentlessly back to the past, to a time when she really had felt like a princess—pampered, sheltered, a popular figure in the social scene of their small Ohio city.

Foolish, she added. *Living in a dream world that was bound to crash.* It had crashed, all right, in a scandal that took away everything she knew.

She took a deep breath and managed to glance at him. He looked hurt.

"I know you weren't happy to see me here, Ellen. I know I let you down. But I'm a different person now."

"I hope so." She did hope it, with all her heart. Maybe that was why she hadn't been able to tell him to go away when he'd turned up after all these years, even though common sense said he'd only bring trouble.

"I've changed," he said, eagerness coloring his voice. "Believe me, prison changes a person."

"Don't." The word came out involuntarily. "Don't, Dad. I don't want to talk about it."

"But, Pr—Ellen, we have to."

"No, we don't." She pulled the car to the curb. "Just promise me you won't do anything to make Quinn Forrester suspicious of you. More suspicious than he already is."

"I told you, Gwen and I are just friends. I find her charming." He glanced into the rearview mirror, straightening the blue tie that matched his eyes.

Charming. Plenty of people had used that word about Charles Wayne, including his daughter. Until the day he was arrested for embezzlement, leaving her bereft and alone, bankrupting herself in a futile attempt to pay off his debts.

There was no time to think about that now, not with Gwen already opening the front door of the rambling Victorian house. Her father took her arm as they got out of the car, and she felt a brief moment's pleasure in his courteous manners.

"I don't care who knows the truth, you know," he said quietly.

Panic shot through her. "Well, I do." She stopped on the walk, turning to face him, and spoke in a furious whisper. "I still feel the pain of what happened back in Winstead when people knew the truth. It took me a long time to find a place where I belong again, and I won't let you ruin it."

He nodded, and for an instant she almost imagined she saw the sheen of tears in his eyes. That was impossible. Charles Wayne took everything in life far too lightly to be brought to tears by her.

"I won't do anything to hurt you, Ellie. You can count on me."

She held back a despairing sigh. She'd counted on him before, and then found out he was living a lie.

"Come right in." Gwen waved them into the wide center hall of the gracious old house, and Kristie danced forward to hug Ellie. "Dinner will be ready in a few minutes."

"Let me help you, Gwen." She was uncomfortably aware of Quinn, standing silent behind his mother. He'd shed his jacket and tie and should have looked relaxed. Instead he looked unyielding. He was only too obviously not joining in the welcome.

"No, no, it's all under way. But I did want to show you those notes about the craft fair. Now where did I put them?" Gwen looked around, her soft rosy face puzzled, as if the papers should spring into her hand.

"You had them on the coffee table, I think," Quinn said. "Why don't you and Ellie take a look at them, and I'll see to things in the kitchen." His smile carried nothing of amusement in it. "Charles can help me."

Ellie had another moment of panic at the thought

of her father alone with that formidable personality, but before she could say anything, Gwen swept Charles toward the kitchen, taking Kristie with them.

"You show Ellie where those notes are, dear. Charles and Kristie will help me."

The kitchen door swung shut, and Ellie thought she heard Quinn grind his teeth in exasperation. Then he gestured toward the living room.

"In here. I think that's where she left them."

She was uncomfortably aware of his tall figure looming over her as she glanced through the notes Gwen had made about the craft fair arrangements. She didn't want to look up at him, but she couldn't seem to help herself. He was frowning, and his gray eyes had taken on the glint of steel. Her heart thumped, and she braced herself for another question about her father.

"It sounds as if you and my mother have taken on a big project."

For a moment she didn't know what he was talking about, and then she realized he meant the craft fair.

"We're cochairing it for the church fund-raising committee. The pipe organ desperately needs a complete overhaul, and we're trying to raise the money."

She'd much rather talk about the fund-raising

project than her father, although maybe in the end it came back to the same thing. She'd conceived the idea of the craft show as a way of repaying her church family for their kindness and acceptance. And she wouldn't have been so desperately in need of that kindness if it hadn't been for her father. But Quinn couldn't know any of that.

She had a crazy desire to laugh at the situation. She was no more eager to see her father involved with Gwen than Quinn was, for several very good reasons. But she couldn't risk ever letting Quinn know why.

"I guess, as the organist, you have a vested interest in that."

She nodded. "It's a fine old instrument, but nothing more than basic maintenance has been done for years. I say a prayer each time I touch it that the mice haven't nibbled on anything crucial."

"You never did tell me where you studied." He slid the comment in casually, but his expression was watchful.

She suppressed a sigh. Quinn wasn't going to give up easily, that was clear, and he wouldn't be content with the carefully crafted version of her past she usually gave when pressed. Somehow she had to convince him that her father didn't represent a threat to his mother.

"Actually I started piano lessons when I was

about Kristie's age. I didn't get interested in the organ until I belonged to a church in Philadelphia. The organist took me under his wing and taught me.''

She sent up a brief, thankful prayer for the elderly man who'd shared more than his love of music. He'd shared his love of God, and his profound faith had brought her out of the spiritual low she'd been trapped in after her father's conviction.

"He meant a lot to you," Quinn said quietly.

"Yes, he did." She stopped on the verge of saying he'd given her back her faith. Quinn didn't merit that kind of confidence from her. She was giving too much away, and he was too observant.

She looked up at him, trying to find something light to say, something that would take them away from dangerous personal ground. She realized in an instant she'd made a mistake. He stood very close to her, watching her intently. That single-minded focus of his was disconcerting. It robbed her of the ability to think.

Quinn frowned, his eyes darkening as their gazes held and they were silent too long. Awareness shimmered between them. Her breath caught. She shouldn't be feeling anything for Quinn. She couldn't. Of all the men in the world, he was the last one she should feel anything at all for.

Chapter Three

"**D**addy, Grandma says dinner's ready." Kristie skipped to them and took Ellie's hand, breaking the spell that held them immobile. "She says I can sit next to you, Ms. Ellie. Okay?"

"That sounds great, Kristie." Feeling released, she turned away from Quinn.

She had to keep her mind on the problem, she lectured herself as Kristie led her across the hall to the dining room.

"Right here," Kristie said, pulling out a chair at the side of the oval mahogany table.

Ellie nodded, slipping into the seat, and then she realized Kristie wasn't the one pushing it in for her. Quinn's hand brushed her shoulder lightly as he settled the chair, and his touch both startled and warmed her. Then he rounded the table to his own seat. Directly opposite her, she saw with a sinking heart.

He sat down, unfolded his napkin, and his gaze met hers over the bowl of zinnias in the middle of the table. How on earth could she concentrate on anything else with him staring at her?

"The roast smells wonderful," she said, wondering how she'd manage to taste it.

"My daddy's favorite," Kristie announced. "We always have his favorite when he comes." Using two hands, she carefully passed the bowl of mashed potatoes to Ellie. "Do you like roast and mashed potatoes, Ms. Ellie?" She looked unaccountably anxious.

"Of course." She took a spoonful, feeling her stomach tighten. This couldn't possibly be a peaceful meal, not with her father beaming at Gwen and Quinn looking like a dam about to burst.

The conversation, accompanied by the clinking of silverware on china, didn't reassure her. Quinn probed into her father's past. Charles parried the questions with his customary skill, but her tension rose with every question, every comment.

How long would it be before her father said too much? She knew how he loved to talk. If he got started on any of his familiar stories, he'd give something away to a listener as acute as Quinn.

"You're going to be here for the craft fair, aren't you, Quinn?" Gwen must have decided that a change of subject was in order. "I'm counting on you to help us out with it."

"I guess so." His gaze turned inward, as if he consulted a mental calendar. "I'm on leave from the project for a month."

Gwen pouted prettily. "You and that project. There's always a new one. This is the first decent vacation you've taken in two years. I'm sure there are plenty of jobs for engineers here in Pennsylvania."

"I have to go where the corps sends me. The work we're doing is important." Quinn sent his mother a quelling look.

"Why don't you work here, Daddy?" Kristie took up the offensive. "Then you could come home every night. You could coach my soccer team, and we could go fishing and you could help with Bible school."

Quinn looked a bit harassed, and Ellie had to smile. Maybe coping with his daughter's wishes would distract him from her father.

"Honey, I can't do that. Not right now. Let's just enjoy my leave, okay? Hey, we haven't talked about your birthday yet, and it'll be here before you know it. Have you decided what you want?"

He wasn't quite as skilled as her father in changing the subject when it got uncomfortable, but he'd probably improve with practice. She found herself wanting to tell him to answer his daughter's question, and reminded herself it was none of her business.

Kristie tipped her head to one side, considering the question. "I want a chocolate cake," she said firmly. "With white icing and lots of sprinkles."

"We can probably manage that," Quinn said.

"And a party with Ms. Ellie and her daddy." She tilted her head toward Ellie. "You'll come, won't you? Please?"

Ellie tried not to look at Quinn, knowing what she'd see in his eyes. "If we get an invitation." He undoubtedly wanted her to make an excuse, but she wouldn't lie to the child.

"What about your present?" Quinn's voice was even, but she could detect tension underneath. "A little bird told me you were thinking about a two-wheeler."

Kristie giggled. "That wasn't a little bird, Daddy. That was me!"

"Oh, yes, that's where I heard it. So, what do you think? Is it going to be a bicycle?"

She shook her head decisively. "I decided there's something I want even more."

Quinn looked surprised, and Ellie wondered if he'd already picked out a bicycle. A six-year-old's wants tended to change from moment to moment, but Kristie would probably be delighted with whatever her father gave her.

"Well, what is it?"

"I don't know if I should tell." Kristie wrinkled her nose. "Do you think it's sort of like wishing on your candles? I mean, if you want something really, really bad, maybe you'll get it if you don't tell."

"If you don't tell," Ellie pointed out, "Daddy won't know where to buy it."

"He doesn't have to buy it!" For some reason, Kristie thought that was hilarious.

A spasm of apprehension crossed Quinn's face. "Even so, sweetheart, I think you'd better tell me."

Kristie considered a moment, then nodded. "Well, see, it's something I was praying about. Ms. Ellie taught us about praying in Sunday school. And she said that God always answers, but sometimes He has to say no." She turned to Ellie. "Isn't that what you said?"

Now she was the one who was apprehensive, Ellie thought as she nodded. What on earth had she said that played into Kristie's birthday wish?

"So I decided I'd ask for it for my birthday," Kristie said confidently. "I always get what I want for my birthday, and if I do that and pray, too, I'm sure to get it."

"I don't think..." Ellie began, then fell silent when Quinn frowned at her.

"So what is it you want?" Quinn looked afraid to find out.

Kristie smiled confidently. "I want you to get married so I can have a mommy. Then you'll come home to stay."

"So, do you think you understand now?" Quinn concentrated on his daughter, seated between him and Ellie on the back porch swing. He tried to ignore the way Ellie's arm curved around Kristie, the way her hand brushed his as she patted the child.

Think about your daughter, he lectured himself. *Not about Ellie Wayne, no matter how attractive she is.*

Now where had that come from? He was *not* attracted to Ellie. Her hair tickled his shoulder, escaping as usual from its band, and the faint scent of roses teased his senses, mingling with the spicy aroma of his mother's marigolds. It looked as if he'd have to keep reminding himself he wasn't.

They'd just tried to explain to Kristie the difference between prayer and birthday wishes, and he still wasn't sure they'd succeeded. Maybe he'd have been better off doing this without Ellie, but he felt she carried some of the responsibility.

"I guess so." Kristie looked up at him with trust

shining in her eyes. "But that's still what I want for my birthday, okay?"

He tried to suppress a sigh of exasperation. "Kristie…" he began, but she slid off the swing and patted his knee like a little mother.

"It's okay, Daddy. You think about it. I'll go help Grandma with dessert while you decide."

She danced across the porch, her white sundress flitting around her. The screen door slammed behind her.

He looked at Ellie. Her expressive face was perfectly grave, but he thought a trace of amusement lurked in her dark eyes.

"I suppose you think this is funny."

Her dimple showed. "Maybe just a bit. She is one very determined little girl. I wonder from whom she inherited that quality?"

She had a point there, though he hated to admit it. Certainly Julie had never been that way. Julie had been sweet, dependent, passive. But never determined.

"Do your spiritual lessons with six-year-olds always end up like this?" He firmly lobbed the ball back into Ellie's court.

Her expression clouded. "I hope not. I take it very seriously, and I try to put things in terms children can understand. But you just never know how they're going to interpret what you say."

"To an engineer, precision is crucial."

"Even when you're dealing with a six-year-old?"

"Especially when you're dealing with a six-year-old like mine." He frowned. Did he really have a clue what Kristie needed anymore? "I already ordered the bicycle. It's hidden over at Brett and Rebecca's house. Bright blue, with streamers on the handlebars."

"She'll love it. Really." She reached toward him, almost as if she wanted to comfort him. Then, just as quickly, she drew her hand back, apparently thinking the better of it. "I'm sure she knows you want what's best for her."

"I hope so." He looked at her, weighing the caring that shone in those bright eyes. He'd like to believe that was genuine. Unfortunately he couldn't ignore the instinct that told him she was hiding something. "I want what's best for my mother, too."

She knew immediately what he was talking about. He could see that in her sudden wariness. Her expression clouded, and she looked down at her hands, clasped in her lap. "Your mother seems to be perfectly happy with her life."

"You look at her as a friend," he said, trying to ignore the way her dark hair curled against the sunshine yellow of her dress. "At least I hope so. I look at her as the mother who's always been protected.''

She bit her lower lip for an instant, then seemed to come to a decision. Her gaze met his with a certain amount of defiance. "I've already told you that she and my father are just friends.''

"Are they?'' After his mother's performance this morning at church, he couldn't believe that.

"Yes.'' She said it so firmly that he thought she was trying to convince herself. "And if it's any satisfaction to you, I don't want to see anything else between them, any more than you do.''

"Why?'' He shot the word at her.

For an instant she looked disconcerted. "Because...because my father will be leaving soon.'' He sensed she edited her words carefully, and wondered what she'd say if she really spoke her mind. "I just don't think it would work out.''

"That's good, because I intend to make sure nothing happens between them.'' He leaned closer, hearing the sudden catch of her breath at his nearness. They were so close he could see the fine vein tracing her temple, the curve of each dark lash. "And since you agree that a relationship between them is a bad idea, you can help me.''

"I don't—I don't think that's necessary.'' She drew back, setting the swing vibrating with her tension.

"I do."

She started to rise, as if to escape him. He caught her hand, holding her still for an instant. He felt her skin grow warm against his palm.

"And I think you do, too," he said.

"I don't know what you mean."

It wasn't the first time she'd said that to him. But this time they both knew it wasn't true. They seemed to be communicating through their linked hands. He felt the determination on his side and just as clearly felt the doubt and fear on hers.

Ellie's eyes widened, telling him the same instinctive knowledge flooded her. The moment stretched, weighted and silent.

She twisted away from him in a sudden movement and hurried into the house, the screen door slamming behind her.

Quinn took a deep breath, looking down at his hand as if it belonged to someone else. He wasn't sure what had just happened here. Maybe Ellie didn't know, either.

But one thing was very clear. He had to detach his mother from Ellie's father, and he had to guard his own emotions while he did so. Because Ellie Wayne had just roused feelings in him he'd never thought to have for any woman again.

Everything was going to be all right. Ellie had told herself that a dozen times by the next morning, and she still wasn't convinced. Her reaction to Quinn rattled her—she couldn't deny that. She just hoped she hadn't let him see how much.

She glanced around the Sunday school room, trying to focus on it instead of the shop. Her part-time help, young Janey Dean, would do fine without her for the mornings this week while she concentrated on vacation Bible school.

She'd pushed the tables to the side so she could set up a pretend camping area in the center for vacation Bible school. The kids would like that. Unfortunately thinking of the children made her think of Kristie, which led her thoughts right back to Kristie's father.

She had to stop this. There was a simple solution to the problem presented by Quinn Forrester. She'd avoid him, and she'd make sure her father did the same.

She knew Quinn's type, only too well. He might stay in Bedford Creek for a time, feeling guilty about his little girl. But then the need to achieve at his job would kick in, and before he even recognized what had happened, he'd be on his way back to the West Coast.

She bit her lip, thinking of Kristie. *Lord, I'm sorry. I'm being selfish. I shouldn't be hoping he goes away soon, not when his daughter wants so much for him to stay. But what can I do?*

There didn't seem to be any good answer to that question, and she suspected her prayers on the subject of Quinn had been a little self-serving.

She just had to stay away from him, she reminded herself firmly. Surely Bedford Creek was big enough to allow that. She'd stay away from him, and everything would work out fine.

The thunder of running feet announced the first arrivals for Bible school, and she turned her mind firmly toward her plans for the day.

Kristie bounced through the doorway with the earliest group, her small face beaming with pleasure. "We're here!" she shouted.

We? Ellie's heart thudded to her toes as Quinn appeared behind his daughter. He paused for a moment, his tall figure framed in the doorway. His faded jeans and white knit shirt were considerably less formal than the suit, dress shirt and tie he'd worn for church. Less formal, she found herself thinking, but not less attractive.

She forced a smile. "Good morning." She turned to the children. "Wow, you're here early. How would you like to help make a mural of Abraham's sheep?"

Luckily everyone would. She got them started with markers on the newsprint background she'd already prepared and steadfastly refused to look at the doorway. He'd go away.

Several sheep later she glanced up, and her stomach clenched. Despite her hopes, Quinn was still there.

Leaving the young artists to their work, she approached him cautiously, realizing she was being ridiculous. He wasn't going to start discussing their parents in the middle of Bible school.

"Kristie's fine," she said quietly.

"I can see that." He didn't move.

What was wrong with him? Didn't he realize parents were supposed to drop the children off and go? "You can come back for her at noon."

He arched his dark brows, as if in surprise. "Come back? I don't need to come back. I'm staying."

"Staying?" She couldn't help the way her voice rose, and she made an effort to control it. She couldn't let the children see what an undesirable effect Kristie's father had on her. "Why? If you're worried about Kristie adjusting to Bible school, you can see she's fine."

"No, of course I'm not worried about her. I know she loves coming here." Quinn's smile seemed tinged with a touch of malice. "In fact, she loves it so much she insisted I come along. She's talked me into helping with Bible school, so we can be together all the time. I'm your new assistant."

Chapter Four

❧

For just an instant Ellie was speechless, and then anger took over. "Don't I have anything to say about who helps with my class?"

"Don't you want me?" Quinn gave her an innocent look that was belied by the satisfaction in his tone. "I thought vacation Bible school always needed extra help. I talked to the pastor about it, and he thought this was a wonderful idea."

Quinn obviously felt he'd covered all the bases, and her temper rose. "Fine." She clipped the word. "Since you want to help, suppose you supervise the class for a few minutes. I think I'd better talk with Pastor Richie myself."

She assumed he'd balk at being left alone with the children, but he just smiled. "Fine." He strolled toward the mural. "Take as long as you want."

Fuming, Ellie hurried down the hallway, passing classrooms whose teachers didn't have to worry about anything more than the lesson. *Or making visitors feel welcome.*

Her fists clenched. They always urged the children to bring a friend to Bible school. How could she turn Quinn away? But how could she possibly work with him?

She caught up with the pastor in the kitchen, where he was arranging trays of cookies and fruit for the children's snack.

"Don't we have a volunteer to do that?" she asked, diverted from her mission at the sight of Pastor Richie in an apron.

The minister's round, cherubic face creased in a smile. "Rebecca volunteered to set up refreshments before she went to the clinic, but she's feeling sick, I'm afraid. I told her we didn't require expectant mothers to help, at least not first thing in the morning." He popped a broken piece of gingerbread in his mouth. "Besides, I'm an expert on cookies."

"Speaking of help…"

He beamed. "Your new assistant, of course! Isn't it wonderful? I could hardly believe it when Quinn said he wanted to work with your class."

"Yes, well, you see…" In the face of the pastor's pleasure, it was amazingly difficult to say she didn't want him. "I'm not sure this will work out. Maybe he'd do better with a different class."

Pastor Richie wiped his hands on his apron, his gaze assessing her. He always seemed able to look right into people's minds, but never seemed surprised at what he found there.

No, not into hers. He'd never guessed the secret she hid, even from him, and for an instant she felt ashamed.

"I'm afraid a different class wouldn't work," he said slowly. "Quinn told me Kristie was counting on his presence. Poor child, she sees little enough of her father."

His words were arrows, hitting her heart. She tried to put up a shield against them. "But surely he'd feel more comfortable working with older children. Or he could help with the games."

Pastor Richie was already shaking his head. "Ellie, please. I realize it may be a little uncomfortable, having the father of one of your students there, but this is a special case. So many of us have been praying for Quinn."

"I know." How could she not? Gwen constantly asked for prayers for Quinn from her prayer partners.

Sympathetic pain flickered in Pastor Richie's eyes. "He's had a difficult time of it since his wife's death, and he hasn't let us minister to him the way we should. Don't you think God expects us to grasp this opportunity to help him if we can?"

He seemed to be putting a charge on her. Much as she'd like to avoid it, she couldn't. She tried to manage a smile. "Yes, of course, Pastor. You're right."

He squeezed her hand. "I knew you'd understand, Ellie. Perhaps God has guided Quinn to a point where he can be helped."

"I don't know that I'm the best person to help him." If the pastor knew why Quinn was here, he'd realize how true that was.

"Nonsense." He squeezed her fingers again. "Your warm heart will tell you what to do and say, my dear. Just follow it, all right?"

This situation had spun entirely out of her control, and she seemed to be out of choices. She tried to smile. "All right. I'll try."

"I don't think that's a good idea." Quinn caught the hand of the little boy who'd apparently decided he could extend the mural onto the wall. "Let's keep the markers on the paper."

The kid stuck his lower lip out. "Don't want to. You can't make me."

Okay, this was the first challenge to his authority as a teacher. Quinn suppressed a ripple of panic at the way all those little faces turned toward him. What had he gotten himself into?

"Then I guess you're finished," he said calmly, and took the marker away.

The boy flung himself into a chair, arms crossed over his chest, scowling fiercely. Quinn looked up to see Ellie in the doorway.

Trying to look as if he knew what he was doing, he strolled toward her.

"Trouble?" she asked in an undertone.

"Just a little marker on the wall." The kid was still glaring at him. "I hope I didn't create more trouble. He doesn't look too happy."

"He'll get over it. A tantrum usually happens at least once a day with Robbie, no matter what we do." She smiled, so apparently Pastor Richie had smoothed things over for him. "We're lucky he doesn't bite anymore."

"Bite? Kristie didn't tell me I should come armed with a muzzle." He discovered he wanted to see her smile more often. It brought out a dimple at the upper corner of her mouth.

"You can always back out if it's too much for you." Her direct gaze challenged him.

That was exactly what he'd been thinking a few moments before, but her words made him perversely determined to stick with it, no matter what. "Not at all. I think it'll be fun."

Was that a shadow of disappointment in her face? If so, she masked it quickly.

"In that case, we'd better wind this down and get on to our story time."

He watched as she gave the children a few minutes to finish what they were doing, then quietly guided them to put materials away. Kristie was among the first to stow her markers in the box, and then she danced over to him and flung her arms around him.

"I'm so glad you're here, Daddy. Are you glad you're here?"

His heart clenched as he returned her hug. "You bet, sweetheart."

No, he wouldn't back out on this. He watched her run back to the group, plopping down on the rug next to Ellie. His helping out this week meant too much to Kristie.

He settled on the floor at the back of the group. Besides, this was a golden opportunity to find out about Ellie Wayne and, by extension, about her father. He watched her draw the children closer to her as she opened the Bible and tried to ignore her soft smile and the way her loving glance touched each little face.

He hardened his heart. He would look at Ellie as if she were a technical problem to be solved, nothing more. By the end of the day, he should know everything he needed to.

The story was God's call to Abraham to set out for a new land. Ellie had a gift for communicating with the children, he had to admit. Her face grew even more animated, her voice changed to depict each character.

The children leaned forward, as intent as if they were watching the latest cartoon or playing a video game. Maybe they were drawn by the power of the story, or maybe by the warmth Ellie projected. Whatever it was, she had them hooked.

As the morning wore on, he found himself wondering how much she needed his help. His mother had assured him that an extra pair of hands was always welcome at Bible school, but Ellie seemed to have everything under control. She moved the class easily from one activity to the next. The most useful thing he'd found to do was to pass out crayons.

Then Robbie planted himself in front of Quinn. The scowl was gone, but the kid's look challenged him. What now? He felt a stir of unease.

"You're Kristie's daddy," Robbie announced.

"That's right."

"Why don't you have red hair like hers?"

This didn't seem the place for a lecture on genetics. "Kristie has red hair like her aunt. I have dark hair like my dad did."

"I don't like red hair."

From the corner of his eye he caught a flash of hurt on his daughter's face. His heart clenched involuntarily, and the depth of his anger astonished him.

Before he could say anything, Ellie steered Robbie back to the table. "God made all of us different," she said calmly. "It would be a pretty boring world if we looked the same. I happen to think Kristie's hair is a beautiful color." She touched her own dark brown curls. "Much more interesting than my plain old brown."

She'd handled it far better than he would have, he realized, and he wasn't sure how he felt about that. If he could, he'd protect his daughter from every bump in the road. Something winced painfully inside him. He'd already learned the hard way how impossible it was to protect the people he loved.

Ten minutes later Robbie was back, and he tensed. But this time the boy didn't look quite as belligerent. "Ms. Ellie says Abraham did what God wanted him to."

"Right." What was driving this kid?

"What I want to know is, how did he know what

God wanted? She says God spoke to him, but I never heard God say anything.''

He longed to look at Ellie for guidance. Or even to have her come to the rescue. But he wouldn't be much of a helper if he couldn't answer a simple question.

"Maybe not with your ears," he said, remembering a long-ago Sunday school class and his own questions. "But what about with your heart?" He touched the child's striped shirt. "Didn't you ever have a feeling right in here that there was something you should do? Or maybe something you shouldn't do?"

Robbie's face clouded. "I guess so. Sometimes."

"We have to learn to listen with our hearts," Ellie said, and he realized she'd caught their exchange, realized, too, that the rest of the class was listening. "That takes practice, but the more you try, the better you'll get." Her gaze met his, and she smiled approvingly.

He began to regret his quick words the day before about teaching spiritual lessons to kids. Maybe he understood her attitude a little better now than he had then. And maybe he'd bitten off more than he should, given his own distance from God in the last two years.

It wasn't until they'd taken the class outside for games that he finally had a chance to talk to Ellie without an audience. Several high school kids had been recruited as game leaders, giving the teachers time to catch their breath.

Ellie sat on the grass under one of the birch trees, her full denim skirt spread around her. He sat down next to her and leaned back on his elbows, surprisingly tired by the morning spent with the kids. And Ellie.

He glanced toward her to find her giving him a measuring look. "How are you holding up? Was it what you expected?" Her earlier anger seemed to be gone entirely.

"Well, it's not quite as tough as building a dam," he admitted. "But almost."

"I'm surprised you were able to take this much time off from your work." She plucked a few strands of long grass, plaiting them without looking, as if her fingers were on automatic pilot.

"I was due some leave." His thoughts flickered to the flood-control project, nearly finished now.

"You don't look as if it was that simple to get away." Ellie plaited a red clover flower into the braid.

"It's never simple." He inhaled the fresh scent of newly cut grass and found himself relaxing. "There's never a good time to get away from a project. That's part of the job."

"I suppose things were easier to handle when Kristie's mother was alive."

For an instant he wanted to flare out at her, to say it wasn't any of her business. But then something—maybe the warmth in her eyes, maybe the cheerful cries of the children playing in the distance and the soft hum of a bee buzzing in the clover—stilled his quick response.

"Not necessarily easier. Julie tried to support my career, but she never wanted to go where the corps sent me."

"That's why she and Kristie came here?"

"She didn't want to go out West." He tried not to sound resentful. "She thought they were better off here, where my family could support her."

He clamped his mouth shut, pressing his hands flat into the warm grass. She probably knew the rest of the story. Julie, driving back from a shopping trip on a rainy night, the drunk driver who'd wiped her out with a careless swerve. Everyone in Bedford Creek knew that.

"I'm sorry," she said, her voice soft. Her hand brushed his with a butterfly touch. "I didn't know her very well, I'm afraid. And I can't say I understand, because I've never lost anyone like that."

He nodded, not looking at her, but somehow soothed. Most people either avoided the subject entirely, as if embarrassed, or claimed they understood. Either response was hurtful, but generally he preferred avoidance. He could manage not to think about Julie when people who didn't know about it surrounded him.

He'd set out this morning to find out more about Ellie. As the children rushed toward them, their playtime over, he realized that he'd just revealed more than he had learned. He wasn't quite sure how that had happened.

"Dad, I'm just too busy to talk now." Ellie hoped she didn't sound as edgy as she felt. She glanced across the counter of the shop at her father late that afternoon. "I know you're trying to help, but I need to balance these books myself."

Her father looked wounded, as if she thought he couldn't be trusted with the shop's accounts. Maybe that was true, but she didn't want to hurt his feelings.

"There must be something I can do to help you. Any errands that have to be run?" Charles brightened a little at the thought. He really seemed to enjoy being out and about in Bedford Creek, accomplishing some small chore. Maybe it reminded him of the days when he'd been known and respected in another place.

Her gaze landed on the poster order for the crafts fair, ready to go to the printer. She'd intended to take it herself, but she'd been busy with Bible school. "Would you like to take this up to the printer's? I've already talked with them about it."

He seized the sheaf of papers. "Of course, Princess. I'll take care of that immediately. You don't need to worry about a thing."

Of course she'd worry, how could she help it? But she managed a smile. "Thanks. That's a big help."

It was much the same thing she'd say to a child who'd offered to erase the board, but her father beamed as if she'd given him a present. Somehow that happiness touched a long-forgotten chord in her heart, echoing with memories of the pride and love she once felt for him.

"Daddy…" The word came out without volition. She slid from her stool and took a quick step toward him, kissing his cheek lightly. "Thanks."

He blinked, then nodded and started out the door, clutching the papers carefully. He paused to hold it for the person who was coming in. Quinn.

Her nerves jangled in tune with the bell over the door. Why was he here? And how much of her confused feelings for her father had been written on her face when he walked in?

"Quinn. I didn't expect to see you again today." That probably sounded unwelcoming.

He'd been watching her father walk jauntily up

the street, but he turned at her words and surveyed her. She resisted the urge to be sure her hair was tidy. It never was, and today wouldn't be any different. Anyway, she didn't care what Quinn thought of her looks.

"Your father helping out with the shop?" He sauntered over to the counter, and she retreated behind it.

"No." She resisted the urge to tell him it was none of his business. That would just make him more interested, if that were possible. "He's taking the craft show posters to the printer for me."

"Must be nice having him around. I understand you hadn't seen each other for a long time." His words were casual, but his gray eyes were alert.

Hannibal, perhaps recognizing Quinn's voice, jumped lightly from the show window to the floor and rubbed against his legs. Quinn bent to scratch behind the cat's ears, giving Ellie a moment to regroup and decide how to respond to his unspoken question.

"My father had been working in another state for several years before he retired," she said neutrally. "Is there something I can do for you?"

He straightened. "I'm here to do the planning for tomorrow."

"Tomorrow?" She looked at him blankly.

"Bible school," he said. "Remember? I know I

wasn't much help today, but I really can do more than just pass out crayons. I thought we could plan the lesson together.''

That was the last thing she'd expected. She'd assumed he wanted nothing more than to be at Bible school with his daughter. That was certainly enough participation to satisfy Kristie.

''That's not necessary.'' She realized that sounded as if she thought he couldn't do it, and embarrassment flooded her. First her father, now Quinn. She seemed to be making a habit of clumsy words. ''I mean, you don't have to do any of the actual teaching.''

He raised an eyebrow, amusement showing in his face. ''Does that mean you think I can't?''

''No, of course not.'' She was going from bad to worse. ''I'm sure you can, but since your aim is to spend time with your daughter, you don't need to…well, do anything more than be an aide.''

''That is what I had in mind originally.'' He leaned against the counter, the movement bringing him closer to her. His long fingers brushed the basket of sachet that sat there, releasing the scent of last summer's roses.

''Well, then…''

''But I've changed my mind.''

She wanted to tell him to change it back, but she could hardly do that. ''Why?''

"Remember Robbie?" He smiled suddenly, his whole face lightening, and her pulse accelerated.

"I couldn't forget him. If anything, I'd think Robbie would make you want to run in the other direction. He usually has that effect on people."

"Tempting," he admitted. "But just for a minute there today I felt as if I reached him. That's a feeling I hadn't had for a while." His mouth quirked a bit, as if he mocked himself. "I think I'd like to feel that way again."

Something squeezed her heart, and she remembered Pastor Richie's words. She'd wanted to reject them at the time, but maybe he'd been right.

Unlikely as it seemed, perhaps God was giving her a chance to minister to Quinn Forrester. Little though she might like it, no matter how dangerous to her secret it might be, she couldn't turn away.

Chapter Five

Quinn waited, watching the thoughts chasing across Ellie's mobile, expressive face. This clearly wasn't how she'd expected things to go, and he suspected she didn't know what to make of it.

Fair enough. That's how he felt about the morning at Bible school. Something about Ellie, maybe the warmth and sympathy she exuded, had changed things between them.

If that warmth and sympathy were real, those qualities should work to his advantage now. She'd have to say yes. He waited, leaning against the counter as if he had all the time in the world.

Finally Ellie nodded, a reluctant smile tugging at her lips. "Okay. If that's really what you want. Believe me, it's harder than it looks. And I can get a bit possessive about those kids. Their spiritual well-being is important to me.''

"You think I'm not up to the challenge?'' He raised his eyebrows. "Think I can't handle it?''

"I think you might be surprised at the questions they ask.''

"You're forgetting, I have personal experience of that with Kristie.''

Not enough, not lately, a little voice whispered in his mind. He thought again of Kristie's birthday wish, and guilt stabbed him. But he couldn't marry someone just to provide Kristie with a mother.

Ellie kindly didn't point out that he hadn't been around to answer many questions recently. "Do you want to work on the lesson now?''

The cat leaped to the counter, and he stroked the animal, wondering if Ellie would try to put him off. "I can come back later, if that's better. I know how hard it must be, juggling the shop and your volunteer work during tourist season.''

Later. He could practically see her mind working behind those dark-lashed eyes. *When her father would be here.*

"No, that's all right. We can do it now. Monday's not a busy day in the shop, and I have a good part-time helper when I need her. Have a seat.'' She gestured toward the round oak table in the corner of the shop. "I'll get my book.'' She spun and disappeared quickly up the staircase, her heels clicking on the bare wooden treads.

One hurdle over, he thought, strolling to the table. He scanned the area behind the counter. Nothing there but business-related things, probably, and he wasn't about to start rifling through her books, even if he thought it would give him answers. Although if he continued to come up blank on the elusive Mr. Wayne, he might be tempted.

The oak table, its surface scarred by years of use, held a scattering of craft supplies. Ellie must have been using the breaks in her day to work on some of the things she sold in her shop. He brushed a skein of yarn from the spot in front of the chair. He hadn't been idle today, either, but she'd probably been more productive than he had.

He'd been trying to find out something—anything—about Charles Wayne. He'd been remarkably unsuccessful. The man seemed to have no history. So he was here, looking for answers.

What he'd told Ellie was true, as far as it went. He did find the kids intriguing. He did want to do something more useful than pass out crayons.

But he had an aim that wasn't quite so altruistic. He intended, one way or another, to find out some concrete fact about the Wayne family. Something, one little bit of information, that would unravel their past and lead him to the truth.

He angled his chair a little closer to the one Ellie had obviously been using. Hannibal twined around his legs, then leaped lightly to the table and nosed inquiringly at a pile of corn husks.

"I don't think she wants you to get into those." Quinn lifted him away and sat down. He thought the cat would escape, but instead it settled on his lap, kneaded his jeans a time or two and purred.

"You're right about that." Ellie crossed to the table, her step light. "I don't know what the attraction is, but every time I work with corn husks, Hannibal tries to appropriate them." She tickled the cat's ears. "They're not on his diet, believe me."

"What on earth can you do with a corn husk?" He watched as she put the book down in front of him, moved her chair an inch farther from him and sat down with a rustle of denim.

Nervous—yes, Ellie was definitely nervous. Her color, always vivid, was a touch brighter, her movements a little quicker. Even her cloud of dark hair seemed to spark with nervous energy, as if it would shock him if he touched it. He suppressed the desire to find out.

"Corn husks? Lots of things." She seemed relieved to talk about a neutral subject.

He was happy to let her. Let her relax, feel at ease with him. Then she might relax her guard enough to say something useful.

"Lots of things like what?" He wasn't really interested in crafts, but it would keep her talking.

"Corn husk wreaths, corn husk flowers, corn husk dolls." She picked up something that had been partially hidden beneath the pile of loose husks. "Like this one."

He took it from her, turning it in his hands. "It's an angel." The tiny halo was braided from corn silk, and the wings cut from a single husk.

"People will start buying now for Christmas." She picked up another one, half-made. "I like to think of my angels on so many different Christmas trees, in so many homes."

He thought again of the way that her hands had caressed the handmade quilt the first time he'd seen her. That hadn't been a salesperson's ploy. She was doing the same thing now, with the half-finished doll.

"You make something out of nothing." He felt a little envious. His job was controlling things, not creating.

She shook her head, smiling a little. "Only God does that. I make something out of things other people would throw away."

"Why?" He wanted, suddenly, to know more than facts about her background. He wanted to know who Ellie Wayne was inside.

"Why?" She looked startled, as if she hadn't

considered the question. "I don't know. I guess because it's satisfying. To take an object someone might consider useless and create a thing of beauty from it might not be great art, but it's creative. It makes me happy."

For a moment they were still, her words hanging in the air between them in the cozy shop. The grandfather clock against the wall ticked, and the cat purred on his lap. *It made her happy.* He'd wanted to know what she was like, and she'd shown him a piece of herself.

Her gaze slid away from his, long dark lashes shielding her eyes. She dropped the doll and picked up the Bible school book. "We'd better get to work."

Before you give anything else away? Is that what you're thinking, Ellie?

She leafed through the book to the lesson for the next day, and he hitched his chair closer to hers. She glanced up, wary again, and he smiled.

"Can't see the book from over there."

"It—it's too bad we didn't order two teacher books for the class. But I didn't expect to have a helper." She spread the book flat and slid it toward him. "Here we are. Tomorrow's lesson is a tough one to teach children. They'll love the story of Isaac's birth, but the sacrifice is hard to deal with."

"Especially at this age." His mind flew, inevitably, to Kristie. "How do you handle it?" He lifted an eyebrow. "You did notice I said 'you.' I'm not going to touch that one."

Her generous mouth relaxed in a smile. "See? I told you it was tougher than it looked."

"Touché." He lifted his hands in a gesture of surrender. "You're the authority. I'm the rank amateur. Give me something I can't mess up."

She nodded, the smile lingering on her lips, and turned to the book.

They worked their way through the lesson, discussing each part, dividing up the responsibilities. With her attention on teaching, Ellie seemed to forget her wariness where he was concerned. She gestured, excited about a concept, laughing over something a child had said about a Bible story.

He liked it, he realized. He liked the way her face lit up, liked the caring that shone in her eyes. That couldn't possibly be faked.

And he liked more than that. That bountiful hair of hers, escaping as always from the tie that was supposed to hold it back, brushed his shoulder. It tickled his cheek when she leaned close to point out the memory verse for the day. Her scent teased him to identify it, something as fresh and natural as she was herself.

She glanced up from the book suddenly, her gaze tangling with his. Her eyes widened as if she'd just read his thoughts, and her hand clenched on the page.

"That's about it," she said quickly. "I can get the activity sheets ready. You don't need to help with that. I'm sure you want to get home."

"Not at all." He smiled blandly. "My mother took Kristie to play with a friend, so I'm on my own until supper. I'll help."

Her hand went down flat on a stack of construction paper. "You don't have to."

"If I can build a dam, I can certainly cut out a camel." He held out his hand for the scissors. "Give me a break, Ellie."

That was just what she didn't want to do—he could sense it. Her mouth tightened a little, but she handed over the scissors without another protest.

"So that is what you do?" She picked up a sheet of construction paper and snipped busily, not looking up at him again. A lock of dark hair fell dangerously close to the scissors blades, and she shook it back. "Build dams?"

"Mostly." He cut carefully around a camel's tail, feeling as if his hands were too big for the scissors. "I do flood-control projects. We're finishing up a big one out West."

"You like it out there." It was a statement, not a question.

He considered. "Like it? I hadn't thought of it

that way. I like the work I'm doing. It's important."
And it keeps me too busy and too tired to feel.

"I guess it must be quite a change from Bedford Creek."

She was leading him to talk about himself to keep the focus off herself, he realized. But there was more than one way to get where he wanted.

"Every place is a change after growing up in Bedford Creek," he said easily. "I didn't realize until I was grown what an idyllic childhood we had here. Safe streets, everyone knew us, we could go anywhere in town and have people around who cared for us."

"That must have been nice." Something wistful touched her voice.

He grinned. "I'd have to say we didn't always appreciate it, not when we were doing something we didn't want to get back to our parents."

"We?" She took her attention off cutting long enough to shoot him a sideways glance.

"My sisters first, then Brett and I after he moved in next door. We were in and out of each other's houses like we lived there."

Her mouth curved in a reminiscent smile. "My friend Libby and I were like that. All those endless pajama parties."

"Guys don't have pajama parties. Not macho

enough. We camped out in the backyard. You still in touch with her?''

"Libby? No.'' There was a pointed finality in the word, along with regret.

"Too bad.'' He kept his tone casual. "Why not?''

"I—we moved away.''

All his senses went on alert. Her tension was palpable. Something about that move was important.

"Too bad. It's tough to move away from your friends. How old were you?''

She shrugged with a pretense of unconcern that didn't work. "Not so young. And not so far away. I was eighteen.''

"That's when you went to Philadelphia?''

"Not right away. I worked in Columbus for a while.''

So, perhaps, that hometown Charles had mentioned was somewhere near Columbus. And she'd left there after something traumatic happened when she was eighteen. Could he risk another question without sending all her barriers up?

"Did your father go to Columbus with you?''

The shutters slammed down on her expression, closing him out. "No.'' She swept a hand across the table, gathering together the animals she'd been cutting out. "I think I'll finish this evening. There's some shop work I really need to get done now.''

She stood, and it was a clear invitation to him to leave.

He got up slowly. So he'd been getting too close, and she didn't intend to let him stick around. His gaze traced the taut line of her neck, the tension that clouded those bright eyes.

"Okay, Ellie. I'll be on my way, then. I'll see you in the morning."

"Fine." She didn't look as if the thought gave her much pleasure.

Actually, what he was thinking wasn't giving him much pleasure, either. The idea that had been floating around in the back of his mind settled into a reluctant certainty.

Ellie was hiding something about herself and her father. She wouldn't tell him what that something was, not of her own volition. So he'd have to do it another way. He'd hire a private investigator to trace Charles Wayne's past.

It was the logical thing to do, he assured himself as Ellie showed him to the door. He had to protect his mother. If the investigation didn't show anything harmful, Ellie need never know about it.

So why did the whole idea make him feel as if he was betraying her?

Ellie pulled the shop van carefully into Gwen's driveway the next afternoon. She'd rather be almost anywhere else than here, where she might run into Quinn yet again. But she and Gwen had arranged to drive to Henderson this afternoon to pick up the display panels for the craft show, and that needed to be done today.

Besides, Quinn probably wasn't here anyway. She'd pick up Gwen and be on her way, with no further chances for him to pick her brains or probe her past or upset her senses with his sheer masculine presence.

Now where had that come from? She wasn't upset by him, not in that way. She couldn't be. She wasn't attracted, didn't find her pulse accelerating when he smiled, didn't feel a flood of warmth when his hand brushed hers.

Yeah, right, a sarcastic little voice in her brain commented.

She turned off the ignition, wishing she could just honk the horn for Gwen. But that would be rude, especially since Quinn was right there in front of her, pulling a weed from the flower bed that overflowed with cosmos, phlox and marigolds.

As she slid from the van he straightened in a swift, smooth movement and stood looking at her. Her heart gave an odd little flutter, and she told it sternly to behave.

After all, they'd spent the morning together at Bible school, and she'd managed to keep working with him strictly businesslike. She wasn't going to let her guard down now.

"Hi. Is Gwen ready?"

He raised an eyebrow, causing another rebellious little flutter. "Ready?"

"We have an appointment to go to Henderson to pick up some things for the craft show." She glanced at her watch. "I'm a few minutes late, I'm afraid."

"She's not here."

She stared at him blankly. "Not here? But we made arrangements ages ago to go to Henderson today."

"She took Kristie shopping." He took a step toward her, and sunlight slanting between the big trees touched his face with gold. "They were going all the way to the mall in Cedarton, so I don't expect them back for hours."

"But..." She forced herself to concentrate on the problem, not Quinn. What was Gwen thinking of?

"Are you sure your plans were for today?"

"Of course I'm sure. We knew it would take two of us to manage the display panels, and this was the only afternoon that suited both of us."

"She'll be upset that she forgot." He frowned, as if it was up to him to solve the problem. "Any chance you can do it tomorrow?"

Frustrated, she shook her head. "We're borrowing them from a gallery there, and it's closed on Wednesdays." She'd have to go alone, that was all.

Quinn brushed off the knees of his jeans and turned toward the porch. "Just wait while I leave a note for my mother."

She blinked. "What do you mean?"

"Isn't it obvious?" He lifted his straight brows. "I'll go with you."

"No—I mean, that's not necessary," she said quickly. She'd manage the job herself, somehow. Anything was better than going with Quinn.

"Don't be silly." Quinn's smile bore a hint of challenge. "You'll just have to make do with a different Forrester, that's all."

"You don't need to do that." The thought of driving all the way to Henderson and back alone with him in the van put a note of panic in her voice.

He ignored her protest. "I'll just be a minute." He took the porch steps two at a time. "Then we can get on the road."

She took a deep breath, suppressing the urge to leap in the van and drive away. Doing that would only make Quinn more suspicious than he already was.

She didn't want to spend the afternoon with him. She was afraid to. But before she could come up with an alternative, he was back.

"Ready?" He looked at her inquiringly.

She swallowed hard, then nodded and climbed back into the driver's seat. Quinn settled next to her, buckling his seat belt, and she started the van.

She backed out of the driveway cautiously, wishing for something that would dissipate her awareness of his solid form, just inches away. Something that would erase the warmth she felt when he glanced across at her. And the flutter of her pulse when he leaned close to switch on the radio, and the spicy scent of his aftershave as it touched her senses.

This had to stop. But she didn't know any way to make that happen. Like it or not, and she told herself fiercely that she didn't, Quinn seemed able to reach past the barriers she'd built around herself. He aroused feelings she'd thought were safely buried. And she didn't know what to do about it.

Chapter Six

❧

"Are you hungry enough to share an extra-large?" Quinn glanced at Ellie across the red-and-white-checked tablecloth. The mingled aromas of tomato sauce and cheese filled the air of the small restaurant in Henderson.

Ellie shrugged, as if unwilling to commit herself. "We didn't need to stop for supper." She'd been saying that for the last fifteen minutes, and he'd been ignoring it just as long.

They'd finished the errands Ellie had to do that afternoon for the craft show. Then he'd spotted the pizza parlor, and he'd realized how long it had been since lunch. He'd overridden Ellie's objections, and here they were.

Apparently giving up the argument, Ellie accepted a menu and flipped it open. She held it between them like a barricade.

"So what's it going to be? Pepperoni or mushrooms? Or are you a nontraditionalist when it comes to pizza? I see they have pineapple."

"Whatever you like." She closed the menu again. "I don't care." It was as if she feared sharing anything personal with him, even her taste in pizza.

"You must care. Everyone has an opinion on pizza." He kept his voice light.

She shrugged. "Okay, mushrooms." She said it as if determined to humor him.

"That wasn't so hard, was it?"

She met his gaze, startled, and he smiled. "It's okay to say what'll make you happy, Ellie."

"I'm already happy," she said quickly. "The panels are just what I hoped. They'll be perfect for the show. I really appreciate your help." Her gaze slid away from his, as if she remembered how reluctant she'd been to let him come.

"Glad to help." That wasn't quite true. To be exact, he'd been glad of an opportunity to be in her company. He'd figured they couldn't possibly do a forty-mile drive together without his learning something useful.

But so far it wasn't working out that way. Instead of probing, he'd found himself relaxing and enjoying the trip. Enjoying her company, without worrying about what he was finding out. When he'd seen the Italian restaurant, it had been too tempting to prolong the enjoyment.

He gave their order to the waitress, trying to shelve any other thought. When the woman moved away, he glanced across at Ellie again. She was busily folding one of the red-and-white napkins.

"What's the matter? Aren't you satisfied with the way they fold those?"

She stared at it, as if she hadn't realized what her fingers were doing. "Sorry." She set the napkin on the table, and he saw that it had been folded into the shape of a rabbit. "I guess I do that automatically."

"Very neat." He tweaked the bunny's floppy ears. "Is there anything you can't make?"

She tilted her head, considering. "Plenty of things, I'm afraid. I can't build a dam, believe it or not."

"But you can turn napkins into rabbits. Where did you learn how to do that? Don't tell me they have napkin-folding classes in school."

She shrugged, a touch of sadness in her eyes. "My mother taught me. She loved doing things like that."

"I thought it was always just you and your father." He thought of Kristie, also motherless, and his heart cramped. Still, she'd found substitutes for Julie in his mother and sisters, hadn't she?

"My mother died when I was eight." Ellie looked almost surprised that she was confiding in him.

"Just a little older than Kristie. Maybe that's why she's grown so fond of you. She recognizes the bond." They had a bond forged of shared experiences and similar pain. "No aunts and uncles and grandparents?"

"Just my father." Her mouth tightened on the words, as if she didn't intend to let anything else out.

"That must have made the two of you very close," he said quietly. For the first time, he wasn't mentioning her father in order to pry. He just wanted—he tried to analyze his motives. The truth was, he didn't know what he wanted. To understand her, maybe.

She seemed to weigh his words for a moment, then nodded. "Yes, we were close. He was everything to me."

Something pained and private showed briefly. He fought against the urge to touch her cheek, to caress that secret grief away.

Instead he wrapped his hand around his glass. That was probably safer. "I guess that's not what my daughter would say about me." Still, it was better, wasn't it, that she didn't have to depend only on him?

"Kristie's luckier than I was." Ellie seemed to hear the concern he didn't want to voice. "She has a loving family to count on, as well as her father. And she knows you love her."

"Does she?" He didn't intend to let his worries about Kristie out, but he couldn't help it.

"Of course she does." She reached across the table, impulsively gripping his hand. Their palms linked, fingers intertwined.

For a moment they looked at each other without barriers, as if they'd known each other a long time and were about to know each other even better. It might have been a moment full of promise, the kind of moment when a man and a woman realize that something good could happen between them.

But it couldn't. He had to remember that. Because just a few short hours ago, he'd hired a firm of private investigators to look into her father's past.

If—when—Ellie found that out, she wouldn't be able to forgive him. And he suddenly realized that mattered far more than it should.

"Do you know you're the most stubborn woman in the world?"

Ellie glanced quickly at Quinn, but amusement

showed in his eyes, not irritation. She relaxed, balancing the awkward panel they were trying to put into the storage closet at the church. Being alone here with Quinn ought to make her wary, but instead it felt as if they'd been working together for years.

"I don't know what's being so stubborn about putting these away. I was sure we'd be able to store the panels here until after Bible school. Maybe it'll go in if we turn it sideways."

Quinn's gaze seemed to measure the panel, then the doorway, and he shook his head. "We can stand it on its head, if you want, but it's not going to fit. You can't put a six-foot panel in a five-foot opening."

"Is that the engineer speaking?"

His sudden smile made her heart contract. "Trust me. I'll get out my slide rule, if you like."

"Not necessary." She gave the awkward-size panel another frustrated push. It bounced harmlessly against the doorframe.

"Stubborn," he murmured again.

"We have to store them somewhere out of the way." She wiped her damp forehead. The August heat had built up in the church since the morning.

He sighed with elaborate patience. "Not even an engineer can fit a six-foot panel—"

"—into a five-foot opening. I know. I got that

part.'' She liked feeling this relaxed around Quinn, liked the way the afternoon had gone. All her fears about this time together had been groundless.

Quinn glanced around the large room. ''Why don't we just prop them against the wall? They won't take up much space.''

''We have Bible school opening exercises in this room, remember? Do you really want them out where the children might knock them down?''

''We could put a Don't Touch sign on them.''

She smiled. ''Would that stop Kristie?''

His baritone chuckle seemed to vibrate in the air between them, almost as if it touched her. ''No, I guess not. Okay, the engineer knows they won't fit in the closet, but the teacher knows they can't be left out. What do we do?''

Again she felt as if they'd been working together comfortably for years. ''Well…'' She glanced around the room, much as he'd done a moment earlier.

The cement block walls didn't offer any answer. But along the far side, a series of coat racks had been installed in wooden frames, forming a wide, high shelf on top. ''What about up there?''

Quinn sized up the shelf, then lifted the panel. ''Looks like it might work. We'll give it a try.''

''Let me help carry that.'' She reached for the end of the awkward panel, but he hefted it easily.

"I've got it. You can bring a chair for me to stand on."

For a moment she stayed where she was, watching the ripple of muscles as he carried the panel across the room. His broad shoulders and lithe movements suggested that he'd managed far heavier burdens.

He put the load down, then looked at her with raised brows. "A chair?"

Sure her cheeks were red, she hurried to drag a metal folding chair across to him. What was wrong with her? She couldn't stand around watching him as if she were a love-struck teenager. All right, he was an attractive man. She'd been around plenty of attractive men without letting it throw her off balance.

Quickly, before he could take it from her, she climbed onto the chair. "You hand them to me, and I'll slide them up."

He frowned. "Maybe I should do that. It's not easy to lift something above your head."

"I'm perfectly capable of doing it. After all, if Gwen were with me, I'd be doing the lifting." She smiled. "Although she'd probably give me an argument."

"She probably would." His frown deepened, but he held the panel up to her. "I don't remember her being quite so assertive in the past."

Perhaps he was beginning to realize that Gwen wasn't the passive, protected mother he remembered. If so, that would be good for all of them.

"Maybe she's grown more independent since your father's death. She's probably had to take care of things she'd never done before."

He paused as he lifted the next panel. "You think that's a good thing?"

Whatever she said, it had to be tactful, bearing in mind his own grief. She breathed a silent prayer for guidance.

"I suppose," she said carefully, "that it can be an example of God bringing good out of something tragic. Your mother didn't need to fend for herself before. But now she's discovered some strength she didn't know she had."

"Maybe," he said, but he didn't sound convinced.

She hesitated, wondering if she should say anything more—that she'd worked with Gwen on committees, that she'd seen her gaining confidence and trying things she hadn't attempted in the past.

But would anything she said end up sounding self-serving? She certainly didn't want to destroy the harmony between them by reminding him of his concerns about her father.

"Will this one fit?" He lifted the last of the pan-

els, and the opportunity slipped away before she
could decide.

"I think so." She eased it onto the stack, shoving
it as far back as possible so there'd be no danger
of them sliding to the floor. "There, that's done it."

"A job well-done." He smiled up at her, the tension around his eyes relaxing. "Congratulations."
Before she could climb down, he grasped her waist
and lifted her to the floor.

Her breath caught. His strong hands held her se-
curely, and she automatically clasped his upper
arms for balance. His muscles felt smooth and
strong under the fabric of his denim shirt.

Don't look up. Don't meet his eyes.

But that caution seemed beyond her control. She
glanced up, to find his face very close to hers. His
eyes darkened. The muscles under her hands tightened, as if he would pull her against him.

Then he snatched his hands away as if he'd
touched something hot. Ellie took a quick step back
from Quinn. Was she crazy? How had she let this
happen?

"Maybe it's time we called it a day," Quinn
said.

"I'll get my keys."

For an instant he looked disconcerted, as if he'd
forgotten he couldn't just walk away from her. "I'd
say I'll walk, but it's getting late."

"Of course I'll drive you." She grabbed her bag and fumbled for her church keys.

Quinn stood waiting while she found them, waited again while she shut off the lights and locked the outside door. They walked across the gravel lot to the van, their steps matching almost as if they belonged together.

No, they didn't belong together. They couldn't, no matter how appealing it might sound.

She stole a quick glance at Quinn's face. She'd been wrong when she told herself there wasn't any tension between them—very wrong. Tension sizzled in the very air when she looked at him.

It had to stop. It had to stop now. She couldn't let herself feel attracted to Quinn—she certainly couldn't let herself get involved with him.

She couldn't be honest with him. And she knew him well enough already to know that was the one thing he'd never forgive.

Ellie pulled into the driveway, coming to a stop near the side door that led into Gwen's kitchen. Thank him, let him out, and then she could go home and give herself a stern talking-to.

"Thanks again for helping me. I really appreciate it."

"It was a pleasure."

Even though she knew it was unwise, she

couldn't keep herself from looking at him. That really was pleasure in his eyes, and it set her pulse fluttering all over again.

She glanced away again, before the moment could become too personal. "It looks as if your mother's home now." Yellow light spilled from the kitchen window in the gathering dusk.

"So it does." He reached across to close his hand over hers on the ignition key. "You may as well come in. She'll want to apologize and explain and hear all about it anyway."

What she ought to do was run the other direction. Instead she found herself switching off the motor, sliding out of the van.

"Just for a moment," she said, falling into step with Quinn again. She wasn't sure whether she was telling him or herself.

He smiled, then touched her waist lightly as if to shepherd her inside when he opened the door.

They took two steps into the kitchen. Ellie felt Quinn freeze behind her.

Gwen sat at the kitchen table, the remains of a meal in front of her. But she wasn't alone. Ellie's father sat next to her, and they looked up with identically guilty expressions.

Her heart thudded to the soles of her feet. Oh, no. Why now? Why, when she and Quinn had grown so comfortable together, did this have to happen? He would think…

Ellie looked at Quinn. If Gwen's expression had been easy to read, Quinn's was even easier. Anger and accusation battled for supremacy. He obviously thought he'd been manipulated, and he'd just as clearly concluded that she'd been in on it.

The accusing look in Quinn's eyes cut Ellie to the heart. For a moment all she could feel was a sense of loss. The rapport that had begun between them had vanished as if it had never been.

Gwen's kitchen should have been a cozy place, with its old-fashioned glass-front cabinets and ivy in brass pots spilling over the shelves on either side of the sink. But the coziest setting couldn't dissipate the tension that crackled from Quinn, and Gwen's guilty expression didn't make things any better.

"What's going on here?" Ice coated Quinn's words.

"Going on?" Gwen's voice rose along with her eyebrows. "Nothing is 'going on.' We're having dessert and coffee."

The mingled aromas of coffee and cherry pie were normally appealing, but they'd lost their charm for Ellie. Her father had let her down once again. She'd asked him not to annoy Quinn further by pursuing his friendship with Gwen. He'd promised to be tactful. And now he'd gone behind her back and done something that made matters worse.

She took a breath, trying to still the tension that crackled along her nerves. Smooth the situation over; get her father out of there. That was the only thing she could do.

Please, Daddy, don't say anything that will rile Quinn even more.

Apparently her father didn't hear her silent plea. He gave Quinn his charming smile and rose, gesturing to a chair. "Won't you join us? I'm sure there's more coffee, and Gwen's pie is wonderful."

Ellie could almost feel Quinn's temper rising at her father's calm assumption of the role of host in his house, and for a second she wondered how she'd become so attuned to him. But this was no time to speculate.

"We'd better get home, Dad. I'll drive you." She didn't want to know what he was doing here, didn't want to know where he and Gwen had been that afternoon. She just wanted to be out of there before Quinn blew up.

"But Ellie, I'm not finished. You can't ask me to leave the best pie I've ever—"

Quinn cut across his praise for Gwen's pie. "Did you forget you were supposed to go with Ellie to Henderson, Mom?" His glare at Charles made it clear whom he blamed for her forgetfulness.

"Oh, my goodness!" Gwen's astonishment would be comical in any other situation. "Oh, Ellie, dear, I'm so sorry. I'm afraid it went completely out of my mind." She got up, fluttering around the table to hug Ellie. "Did you go and get those panels all by yourself? My dear, you shouldn't have."

"No, she didn't." Quinn's exasperation seemed to mount. "She was counting on you, and you weren't here. So I went with her."

"You did?" Gwen's round face creased in a smile, and she reached up to pat his cheek. "That was so sweet of you, dear. Well, it's all taken care of, then, and no harm's been done."

She turned away, seeming to consider the matter ended. For an instant, Ellie glimpsed a self-satisfied expression on her face, as if things had worked out just as Gwen intended, and a little jolt of tension pricked her. What was Gwen up to?

"Mom, that's not the point. You were supposed to help Ellie."

Gwen raised her eyebrows in surprise. "But Quinn, didn't you enjoy going with her?"

Ellie could only be glad the question hadn't been directed at her. She couldn't admit how much she'd enjoyed the afternoon in Quinn's company. The memory of those moments in Fellowship Hall flooded through her.

"Dad, I think we should leave now." She

nudged her father, but he was doing a fine job of remaining oblivious to her hints.

Quinn's brows lowered as he glared at Charles, who got up from his chair. "Perhaps that would be a good idea. My mother and I need to talk."

That seemed to dent Charles's armor. His smile faltered, and he took a step.

"Quinn!" Gwen put a protective hand on Charles's shoulder. "That's no way for you to talk to a guest in my house. I'm ashamed of you." She looked like a pretty ruffled hen, shaking her finger at Quinn as she must have done when he was ten.

"Really, Gwen, we have to leave." Ellie tugged on her father's arm, trying to suppress a totally inappropriate desire to laugh at the ridiculous situation. She and Quinn were united in one thing—they both wanted her father out of Gwen's kitchen immediately.

"Mother, I'm only trying to do what's best." Quinn sounded as if he'd gone too far and knew it.

"I'm perfectly capable of deciding what's best for myself, and so is Charles." Gwen's rare temper had been thoroughly roused. "You children have no business interfering."

Ellie's gaze met Quinn's. For a fraction of a second they shared a blend of exasperation and amusement, as if they were partners, colleagues. Friends. Then Quinn's eyes turned frosty as he seemed to remember that she was the cause of his predicament.

Charles finally moved, and she hustled him toward the door. "We really must be going." She glanced at Quinn, wanting to say... But what could she say? Nothing that would change his mind about her father, probably. "Thank you for helping me today."

Her father was finally out of the kitchen, but before she could follow him, Quinn's hand closed around her wrist. His fingers were warm and strong.

"We need to talk about this." His low voice made the words for her alone.

She tried to pin a smile to her face. "I'll see you tomorrow. At Bible school."

He nodded curtly, then turned toward his mother. Ellie escaped into the evening air.

There wasn't going to be anything pleasant about that conversation tomorrow, she could be sure. All the progress they'd made that afternoon had disappeared. She and Quinn were on opposite sides of a yawning chasm, and nothing was ever likely to bridge it.

Chapter Seven

Quinn leaned against the birch tree in the church-
yard the next day, watching as Ellie put a platter of
peanut butter and jelly sandwiches on the picnic
table. The Bible school children were staying for a
picnic lunch, further delaying any opportunity to
catch Ellie alone.

He moved restlessly, feeling the rough bark
through the fabric of his shirt. He'd thought it
would be easy to have a private conversation with
Ellie. He'd also thought it would be easy to give
his mother advice. It seemed all his assumptions
were wrong.

Across the table from Ellie, his mother poured
lemonade into paper cups for the children. Her
round face wore its familiar serenity. Everything

about her was the same as it had been for years, and yet something vital had changed. She seemed to have developed a different personality since his father's death.

Ellie's words about Gwen discovering her own strength filtered into his mind, and he frowned. He didn't want to take advice about his mother from Ellie, of all people. Not even if he thought she had a point.

He'd tried to talk to his mother after Ellie and Charles had left the night before, but it had been useless. First she ignored his concerns, angry at what she called his interference. Then, when her anger cooled as quickly as the coffee on the table, she tried to talk about adjusting to the death of a spouse—her own, and his.

He pressed so hard against the tree trunk that it was probably leaving ridges in his skin. He couldn't do that. After all this time, he still didn't want to talk about Julie's death. Maybe some people coped with tragedy by discussing it, but he wasn't one of them. His mother, of all people, ought to know that about him.

It was easier to concentrate on his worries about Gwen, and certainly easier to blame Ellie and Charles. Fair or not, that was how he felt.

He watched Ellie again, as he'd been doing all morning. She bent over the table to cut a sandwich, and that untamed hair of hers swung in front of her face like a veil. She turned toward Kristie, laughing at something his daughter said, and his heart clenched at the sight of Kristie laughing back at her.

Ellie had a smile and a quick word for everyone at Bible school, it seemed. Everyone but him, that is. Oh, she'd been perfectly polite all morning. She'd also avoided any opportunity to share a word with him. She'd effectively frozen him out, looking through him as if he weren't even there.

Ellie picked up the empty lemonade pitcher and turned, making some comment to his mother. She walked quickly toward the building. Quinn pushed away from the tree. Like it or not, she had to talk to him. He was through being ignored by Ms. Ellie. He crossed the lawn and went after her.

The church basement was dim and cool after the bright summer sunlight. He stood for a moment, letting his eyes adjust, and then saw the door to the kitchen whisper shut. Ellie had obviously gone for more lemonade. The church kitchen would be a private setting for the conversation he intended to have with her.

She was turning away from the refrigerator with a full pitcher in each hand when she saw him. Her expressive face tightened, and for just an instant he wanted her to look at him the way she did everyone else—with caring and laughter lighting those dark eyes.

He dismissed the thought. No, that wasn't what he wanted from Ellie. He wanted answers.

She put the pitchers down, and they clanked on the long metal table. She stared at him defiantly. "Well, go ahead. Get on with it."

"With what?" He moved closer, watching her hands clench into fists at his approach. "Do you really dislike me that much?"

She looked at him blankly, and he touched her closed fingers.

"You look ready for a fistfight."

"I don't fight." She took a deep breath, opening her hands and lifting them, palms up. They were long-fingered, strong hands—a craftswoman's hands. "I suppose you want to talk about our parents again."

"No." His quick, negative answer obviously surprised her. It surprised him even more. What was he saying? That was why he'd come after her, wasn't it? "Not right now," he added.

She eyed him warily. "You had a reason for following me in here, I suppose."

"I want to know what happened to our working together."

"I don't know what you mean." She turned

away, tracing a bead of moisture as it traveled down the outside of the pitcher.

"You know exactly what I mean." He leaned his hip against the metal table, close enough to touch her if he moved his hand even slightly. "We're supposed to be working together on Bible school."

"Aren't we?" She still didn't look at him.

"Come on, Ellie. You kept me so far from the action today I might as well have been in Siberia."

The small dimple at the corner of her mouth made an appearance. "It wasn't that bad."

"It was worse." He gave a mock shiver. "I'm still cold."

She did look at him then, the smile taking over her face. "I guess I could have involved you more."

"We're supposed to be partners, remember? Helping each other."

Her smile stilled, and she gave him a frank look. "Are you talking about Bible school? Or about our parents?"

It was no good. He couldn't treat her as a friend, not when he was paying a private detective to investigate her and her father. For a moment he considered telling her that, telling her that if she had something to hide she might as well level with him.

He couldn't. His mother's happiness came first;

it had to. He couldn't risk jeopardizing that on someone he didn't even know.

"Maybe both," he said lightly, wondering how she'd react.

She looked up at him with a flash of anger. "I'm sorry if I didn't let you participate this morning. I'll do better tomorrow."

"And the other?"

She stiffened, and he felt the barriers she put up against him. "I told you before I don't want to see a relationship between my father and Gwen. But I can't keep him on a leash."

That was just about what he wanted her to promise him. The realization made him angry, whether at himself or her he wasn't sure.

"I want your promise there won't be a repeat of yesterday," he said shortly. "No more little excursions with my mother."

She lifted her chin. "There won't be if I can prevent it. I'm afraid you'll have to be content with that." She picked up the pitchers and brushed past him, the kitchen door swinging in her wake.

He looked after her. Content? That wasn't a state he'd enjoyed much lately, especially where Ellie Wayne was concerned. But at least he'd gotten her reluctant promise to cooperate.

That was what he wanted. So why didn't it make him any happier?

* * *

What had she expected? Ellie tried to control her hurt and anger as she carried the lemonade out to the picnic table. That one pleasant afternoon together would make Quinn's suspicions vanish? It was absurd. And yet that seemed to be exactly what she'd expected. Or maybe what she wanted.

She pushed that thought away firmly. There was no possible point in thinking she and Quinn could be friends, let alone anything more. She remembered, only too well, what happened to her last relationship when the man she'd thought herself in love with had found out her father was a criminal. He hadn't been able to get away from her fast enough. She didn't intend to repeat that experience.

And with Quinn—for a moment she looked at herself clearly, and was horrified at her own weakness where that man was concerned. Quinn was the last person in the world she could care about. With that iron determination of his to protect his mother, he wouldn't hesitate to make the Wayne family scandal public.

She knew only too well what would happen next. She'd already been through it. The people she thought were her friends, people she loved like family, would look at her as if she were a leper.

A shiver ran along her skin in spite of the summer warmth. She couldn't go through that again.

Somehow she had to deflect Quinn's interest in her father.

Her gaze rested on Gwen, who was clearing the table as the children ran off for games. If she could show Gwen how uncomfortable the situation made her, maybe she'd help. All Gwen had to do was convince Quinn she wasn't falling for Charles Wayne, and the entire problem would disappear.

With a fresh surge of determination, Ellie started toward Gwen. Almost as if she wanted to elude her, Gwen scurried around the far end of the table.

"Gwen."

Gwen stopped, reluctantly it seemed, at the sound of her name. "What is it, Ellie? I want to take these plates to the kitchen."

"That can wait a minute, can't it? I need to talk with you."

Gwen shrugged, her round blue eyes looking everywhere but at Ellie. "I think we really should get the cleaning up done."

Ellie took the plates firmly from her hands and set them on the table. "Gwen, we need to talk."

That was what Quinn kept saying to her, and she wasn't any happier to hear the words than Gwen seemed to be. But she had to push on.

"I'm sorry Dad caused a disagreement between you and Quinn last night. That shouldn't have happened."

Gwen's rosebud mouth tightened. "It wasn't your father's fault, so don't blame him. I invited him to go shopping with us."

That was what her father had said, and she felt guilty for having doubted him. "You know, my father never stays long in one place. I imagine he'll be leaving Bedford Creek quite soon."

"All the more reason to make his visit a happy one." Gwen's tone was righteous.

"Well, of course. But your son won't be here for an extended time, either. You should be spending your time with him."

Gwen's frown disappeared. "Now, Ellie, I just know Quinn enjoyed the day with you far more than he'd have liked shopping with me. And didn't you have a good time with him?"

"It was very nice." She said it with as little enthusiasm as she could manage. Gwen didn't need to know just how nice it had been. "The point is that Quinn really doesn't like your relationship with my father. You don't want to upset him, do you?"

Gwen waved that off. "Quinn can stand to be upset. He takes too much for granted. Besides, it will do him good to be worried about something that will keep him in Bedford Creek." She scooped the dishes from the picnic table and darted off before Ellie could say another word.

Maybe she wouldn't have had a response if

Gwen had given her more time. What on earth did Gwen mean by that? Was she deliberately using the situation with Charles to keep her son in town?

No, that was ridiculous. Gwen wouldn't do that. But their conversation that night at dinner flitted through her mind. Gwen clearly thought it was time Quinn came back to Bedford Creek to stay. What might she do to accomplish that aim?

Ellie worried at it as she finished clearing the table, stuffing the used paper plates and cups into the trash can. Maybe she should ask Gwen point-blank if that was what she had in mind.

She'd almost screwed up her nerve to do that when Gwen came back from the kitchen, but before she could get the words out, Kristie came skipping to her grandmother.

"Grammy, guess what?"

"What, sweetheart?" Gwen put her arms around the child.

"Ms. Ellie told us a neat story this morning. It was all about how God picked out a wife for Isaac. He sent this servant, see, and when the man saw Rebecca, he knew she was the one God wanted."

It was nice to know someone had been listening to the story. She'd been so aware of Quinn's unblinking stare while she was telling it that it was a wonder she hadn't married Rebecca off to the servant.

"So I was thinking about when I prayed for God to give me a new mommy." Kristie wiggled her way free of her grandmother's arms. "I think God picked out a wife for Daddy, just like he did for Isaac. And I think the one he picked out is Ms. Ellie." Kristie beamed in satisfaction. "Don't you think so?"

The paper plates and cups Ellie was holding dropped from suddenly nerveless fingers. *Oh, no. This couldn't be happening. Kristie couldn't possibly have come up with a conclusion like that.*

But she had. And what was worse, Gwen smiled at her as if she agreed.

Lord, what am I going to do now? The only worse thing would be if Quinn had heard that.

She turned, hoping to escape before Kristie realized she was there. And found Quinn standing right behind her.

Ellie felt as if someone had dropped her into a vat of boiling water. Her cheeks burned, and all she wanted to do was run and hide.

She couldn't. She was an adult, and adults didn't do things like that. She had to pin a smile on her face and figure out how to deal with this, no matter how embarrassing it was.

If Quinn had heard… Well, if he'd heard, surely he'd understand. Kristie's longing to have a mother wasn't a secret.

"Ellie, is something wrong?" Quinn's straight dark brows drew into a frown.

"Wrong?" she echoed. Was it possible he hadn't caught his daughter's little bombshell?

"You look as if—" He stopped, shrugged. "I thought you looked upset about something."

He must not have heard. He wouldn't be able to hide his reaction to that. She managed to breathe again.

"You mean about something else besides your obsession with keeping our parents apart?" She might as well go on the offensive. Trying to avoid the subject hadn't done her any good.

For an instant she thought he'd flare out at her, but then his mouth tightened, and he nodded. "Yes. Besides that."

Your daughter thinks God picked me out to be your wife. Well, no, she didn't want to say that.

"No, I'm fine." She sent a cautious glance over her shoulder. Gwen was still talking with her granddaughter, but at any moment she might look their way. Ellie could imagine her calling out.

Oh, Quinn, Kristie just said the cutest thing.

Could this situation get any worse? She walked away from the picnic area, forcing Quinn to move with her if he wanted to continue the conversation. They stepped from shade into sunlight, and she blinked, her eyes dazzled. Quinn seemed to loom like a dark shadow between her and the sun.

"Was there something else you wanted?" Her mouth went dry. She'd gotten him out of range of his mother at the cost of being alone with him herself.

He shook his head. "Guess tomorrow at Bible school we can decide what time I'm picking you up."

"Picking me up?" She had the sense that she'd walked onstage in a play and didn't know her lines. "Why would you be picking me up?"

Now it was Quinn's turn to look confused. "Aren't we going up to White's Woods to gather something or other you and Mom need for the craft show?"

"What makes you say that?" This conversation went in more circles than a top. "Yes, Gwen and I intended to gather some wildflowers and cones, but I had no idea you planned to go." That sounded very unwelcoming, but she couldn't help it.

"Kristie said we're all going."

"When did Kristie tell you that?" She had a sinking feeling she knew the answer before he spoke.

He shrugged. "Just after story time this morning. What difference does it make? At least it'll give my mother something else to think about…"

He let that trail off, but she knew how that sentence would end. Besides her father. That was what he wanted to say.

She was a little more concerned with what Kristie was thinking right now. Kristie had probably decided this expedition was a perfect chance to help God along with what she'd decided was His plan.

"I'm not sure that's a good idea."

"Why not?" That stubborn jaw hardened. "I think right now it's a very good idea for me to stick close to my mother."

Why not, indeed. If she told him what Kristie had said—no, she couldn't do that. It would be far better to discourage Kristie gently in private rather than to make a big deal out of an innocent childhood wish. But if she didn't tell Quinn, she had no good reason for avoiding the expedition together.

It looked as if she'd have to give up on this one. "I have to spend some time in the shop or my helper will feel overwhelmed. Let's make it around four, all right?"

Quinn nodded, then started back toward the church. She watched his tall figure until it disappeared into the building.

Another afternoon spent in Quinn's company, another time of keeping up her guard, trying not to let him see into her secret life. This was a bad idea.

So why did she have to try so hard to squash the soft voice inside her that insisted spending time with Quinn was exactly what she wanted, no matter how unwise?

Chapter Eight

"I'm glad we're going with Ms. Ellie, Daddy."
Kristie wiggled in her seat belt, peering out the window as they approached Ellie's shop the next afternoon. "Aren't you glad?"

"I guess so." That didn't sound very gracious.
"Sure," he added, and pulled to the curb.

Ellie came out so quickly, she must have been watching for them. She slid into the back seat before he could get out to open the door for her, plopping a large basket on the floor. Then she obviously registered the fact that someone was missing.

"Hi." She glanced from him to Kristie. "Where's Gwen? I thought she was coming."

"So did I." He suspected his exasperation showed in his voice. His mother and daughter had gotten him into this little adventure, and then his mother had backed out. Still, she'd had a good reason.

"Rebecca was feeling pretty rocky today, and the receptionist at the clinic didn't show up. Mom went to help out."

"I see."

Her candid gaze told him she wondered why he'd come in that case, but he didn't have a good answer. "Mom said you needed to do this, and Kristie was looking forward to it." He'd just given her two reasons instead of one—always a bad sign.

He didn't have to explain himself to Ellie. He made a careful U-turn in front of the police station, then started up the steep street that headed toward the mountain ridge. He didn't have to explain himself to anyone. His mother was safely involved at the clinic with Rebecca. There was no reason not to be here with Ellie.

No reason to be with her, either, a skeptical little voice in his mind pointed out. He'd heard a brief preliminary report from the private investigator that morning. When he'd mentioned trying to find out more himself, the man had politely told him to leave it to the professionals. They'd come up with any answers that existed.

He glanced into the rearview mirror. Ellie leaned forward, talking to Kristie about the Bible school program set for the next day. Her hair, escaping from its band as usual, twined on his shoulder and feathered against his neck.

So far, their investigation had focused on Ellie's history, since he'd had little to provide them about her father. He'd known she'd worked in a craft shop in Philadelphia for four years before coming to Bedford Creek to open her own shop, apparently drawn by less expensive property here.

The man had commented that she'd appeared to arrive in Philly from Ohio with nothing—no belongings, no furniture and very little money. She'd lived in a cheap, dreary, furnished room for over a year before she'd apparently made enough to get something better.

It only raised more questions. Ellie was obviously well educated. Anyone talking with her for more than a few minutes would, in spite of her propensity for casual, sometimes offbeat clothing, place her as upper middle class. So why had she been practically destitute?

"Turn right just ahead." Ellie touched his shoulder, pointing to the dirt lane half-hidden by a tangle of rhododendron bushes.

"I remember." He slowed, taking the turn onto the rutted lane slowly. He remembered. White's Woods was a local landmark—several acres of meadows, woods, a quarry—that had been a popular spot for hiking and picnics for a couple of generations. "My mother says my father proposed to her up here."

"Really? That's so sweet." They jolted over a pothole, and Ellie grasped his shoulder in an automatic reflex. She snatched her hand away immediately, but the imprint of it seemed to linger. "It's nice—" She stopped, as if she'd been about to say something unwise.

"What's nice?" He negotiated the curve into the meadow and parked by the rough-hewn picnic table that had been there as long as he could remember.

"That sort of tradition, I guess." For an instant Ellie's gaze seemed to turn inward. "Having a place that hasn't changed in so many years."

Isn't there a place like that in your life, Ellie? Before he could ask the question, Kristie opened her door and slid out.

"Hold it," he ordered, grabbing the bag his mother had provided. "You need bug repellent on first, before you go anywhere."

Kristie pouted. "I don't want to. It smells bad." She wiggled. "Don't want to wear this shirt, either. I'll be hot." She plucked at the long-sleeved shirt he'd insisted she put on.

"You'd feel even worse if you got stung by a bee." He tried to say the words lightly, but the memory of Kristie's terrible allergic reaction to a bee sting months ago haunted him.

"I'm wearing long sleeves, too, Kristie," Ellie said, getting out of the car. "I'd never go out in the woods without them." She wore jeans, hiking boots and a long-sleeved checked shirt that looked like a man's, except that there was nothing masculine about the way it looked on her.

Ellie smoothed some repellent on herself, then rubbed the rest of it on Kristie's neck. She glanced up at him. "I have an Epi-Pen in my basket," she said softly.

He had one, too, of course, but he was unaccountably touched that she was so prepared. "Guess we're ready, then. What's first?"

"I want to see the quarry." Kristie grabbed his hand. "Please, Daddy. Grammy wouldn't take me the last time we came. She said she didn't like it. But I want to see it. Please, can I?"

He tried to ignore the tension that knotted his nerves at the thought of the abandoned quarry. No sense infecting Kristie with his own feelings.

"Just a quick look. Then we have to get to work. This trip is business, remember?"

She nodded, red curls bobbing. "Okay."

They cut across a corner of the meadow, passing a stream bordered by river birch and weeping willows, and followed the path through the stand of hemlocks. Ellie walked ahead of him. She'd taken Kristie's hand, and maybe that was just as well. He'd probably hold on to her too tightly.

The path ended abruptly, and Ellie stopped. The quarry yawned ahead of them, a vast gash in the peaceful landscape. Ellie drew his daughter close to her. He came to stand next to them and couldn't help grasping Kristie's shoulder. She was several feet from the edge, but it still set his nerves vibrating.

"It's deep." Kristie leaned forward against their restraining hands. "Is there water at the bottom?"

His gaze traced the rock wall down to its base. The water was so clear it seemed he could count every pebble on the bottom. "Some. Not much now, but if there's a lot of rain, it fills up fast."

Kristie glanced up at him. "Could you go swimming there?" She'd just learned to swim, and she tended to ask that question about every body of water she saw.

"No." It came out too sharply, but he couldn't help that. "It's a dangerous place, honey. Lots of rocks and holes. Nobody should ever swim there."

Or climb there, or do anything else there. He'd nearly lost three friends in that quarry, and that wasn't something a person forgot easily. A few scraggly trees clung to the lip of the cliff, and he could almost picture Brett, half-drowned and exhausted, hauling himself over the edge by grabbing one.

"Come on." He took Kristie's hand, reassured by the way it curled trustingly around his. "We have a job to do. Let's get to work."

He'd meant that lightly, but he soon discovered that it really was work. Ellie had a very specific agenda, and she'd come as prepared to find what she needed as if she were shopping in the supermarket. Not just any flowering plant, or leaf or fern would do.

"Now look at this one." She spread a maple leaf out on her palm, smoothing the edges. "See, it's perfect. We'll use these for the leaf prints we're making with the kids tomorrow. Believe me, if they can argue about who has the best leaf, they will."

He thought of some of the disputes he'd refereed during Bible school and nodded. "Guess you're right. Okay, perfect leaves, coming up."

"Grammy says she wants flowers to dry," Kristie said. "Can I pick some?"

"We'll get those in the meadow," Ellie said. "They don't grow here where it's shady. Why don't you look for cones? You should find some under the trees along the path."

"Okay." Clutching her own small basket, Kristie darted toward the thick growth of hemlocks that overhung the path.

"I'm ashamed to admit I don't know, but why is my mother drying flowers?" Maybe the truth was that he didn't know a lot about what his mother was doing these days. "Don't teenage girls do that? I remember when every volume of the encyclopedia held a rose Angela or Rebecca was pressing. Made it tough to look anything up."

Ellie put a fern frond into the basket. "Your mom and I do a lot of crafts together, once tourist season is over and I'm not so busy. This fall we plan to make dried-flower pictures." She smiled. "You can probably expect to get one for Christmas, if hers turn out the way she wants."

"That should fit very nicely into the décor of the mobile home where I live out on the Oregon woods. It's kind of spartan rustic."

"You expect to be back there at Christmastime, then."

"Did I detect a note of criticism in that comment?"

She shrugged, not looking at him. "It's not my place to criticize."

Before he could agree with her, Kristie ran back to them. "We're almost at the meadow, Daddy. Now can I pick some flowers?"

He suppressed the urge to keep her by his side. He hadn't been brought up that way, and it wasn't fair to overprotect Kristie, either.

"Okay. But stay where I can see you. And don't go near the stream."

Her nose wrinkled. "But Daddy, how do I know you can see me?"

"If you can see us, then we can see you." Laughter threaded Ellie's voice. "Okay?"

"Okay." Kristie darted off, basket swinging so vigorously that several leaves dropped out.

He shook his head, smiling reluctantly. "She makes me laugh about every minute and a half, even when I'm worrying about her."

"Kristie's one of a kind. I guess all the children are, but I have to confess, she has a special place in my heart."

Ellie meant that, he realized. She cherished each one of the kids who came under her care. He'd seen that every day at Bible school, but the depth of her caring still surprised him. That warm heart of hers seemed to embrace everyone in town.

"I'm glad." He stopped, looking down at her. "Glad that Kristie has you."

For an instant there was something questioning in her dark eyes, but then she nodded. "And I'm glad to have her in my life."

She stood looking up at him. A shaft of sunlight wavered through the moving branches overhead. It touched her cheek, illuminating the warm color that flooded her skin, the sweep of thick dark lashes, the pulse that throbbed at the delicate curve of her temple.

Her skin couldn't possibly be as soft as it looked, could it? As if moving of its own volition, his hand lifted. He stroked the line of her cheek, feeling the smooth warmth like silk beneath his hand. Her eyes darkened, and her lips parted. He wanted—

"Daddy!" Kristie's shout was followed by a shriek, then a splash.

Shock flooded Ellie—shock and fear. Quinn snapped away from her as if he'd been shot, and in an instant they were both running toward the stream.

Please, God, please, God. An incoherent prayer thudded in time with her racing steps over the rough ground. She stumbled once, and Quinn surged ahead of her. By the time she recovered her balance and hurried down the bank to the stream he was already ankle-deep in the shallow water.

Kristie, wailing, was on her hands and knees, her face muddy. He scooped her into his arms and carried her to the bank.

"Kristie, are you all right? Are you hurt?" His face was blanched with naked fear.

Ellie reached them and knelt beside the weeping child. "Kristie, honey, stop crying." It took an effort to keep her voice calm. "We need you to be a big girl and tell us if you're hurt.'' She wiped the mixture of tears and mud from Kristie's cheek with her hand. "Come on, now."

Kristie gulped and swallowed a sob. "I—I'm wet!"

Some of Ellie's fear subsided. "We know you're wet, honey. But are you hurt?"

Kristie looked down at herself. "My new jeans are all muddy," she said in a tone of outrage.

"The jeans will wash." Quinn sat down abruptly, as if his legs wouldn't hold him up any longer, and pulled his daughter into his lap. "Now, listen to me, Kristie. Does anything hurt?"

Kristie's lower lip came out in a pout. "No. But my new jeans are muddy."

Quinn's gaze met hers over his daughter's head, and his lips twitched. "That seems to be a recurring refrain."

Ellie smiled, relief sweeping through her. "I think that's a good sign."

"It doesn't explain what Kristie was doing in the creek." He held his daughter back so that he was looking in her face. "Kristie? Didn't I tell you not to go near the creek? Or out of sight?"

She sniffled. "I know. But Daddy—"

"Don't 'but Daddy' me. I want to know why you disobeyed."

"But I was just trying to help." Her voice quivered.

"Help who?" Quinn looked around, as if looking for someone in need.

"Help you and Ms. Ellie."

"I don't understand."

Quinn might not understand, but Ellie began to fear she did. If Kristie meant what she thought she meant, this was going to be uncomfortable.

"Remember the Bible story yesterday? About how God picked out Rebecca for Isaac to be his wife?"

Quinn nodded, still obviously puzzled.

"Well, you need a new wife, and I decided maybe God picked out Ms. Ellie to be her." Kristie clasped her hands together. "I was helping by letting you be together without me. So maybe you'd kiss Ms. Ellie."

She couldn't possibly look at Quinn. Maybe she'd never be able to look at him again—or at least not until the memory faded of that moment when they were standing in the meadow, and she'd thought that kissing her was exactly what he planned to do.

She heard Quinn give an exasperated sigh. "Kristie, what am I going to do with you? I told you. I'm not looking for a new wife."

"But if God picked her out for you—"

"Kristie, you don't know what God intends." Ellie breathed a quick prayer for the right words. "None of us does. Just because you want a new mommy, you can't decide that's what God has in mind for you."

Kristie grabbed her hand in a wet, muddy grip. "But don't you like my daddy, Ms. Ellie?"

She kept her gaze fixed on the child's face and willed her voice to be steady. "Of course I do. But that doesn't mean I'd be the right wife for him. That's something you have to let your daddy decide."

Quinn stood up, carrying Kristie with him. "We'll talk about this some more later, okay? Right now we need to get you home and into some dry clothes."

"But I don't want to go home!" That brought a fresh spate of tears.

Ellie patted her. "We can come again another day. The flowers will still be here."

"Promise?"

"I promise." But she wasn't sure the next outing would include Quinn.

Kristie wiggled. "I can walk, Daddy. Let me down so I can walk."

He put her down. She took a couple of steps, then stopped and giggled. "My shoes squish. Look, Ms. Ellie, my shoes squish." She danced ahead of them.

"I think she's recovered," Ellie said.

"I haven't." Quinn drove his hand through his hair. "She's going to turn me gray."

"I'm sorry I didn't tell you." The words came out impulsively, and then she stopped.

"Tell me? How could you tell me?" He looked down at her, and his expression slowly turned cold. "You knew what she was thinking."

"I'm sorry." She could feel herself flush. "I heard her tell your mother yesterday at Bible school. I thought it would be better—"

"You thought?" He didn't raise his voice, but it was cold enough to send a chill down her spine. "Seems to me you didn't think. Kristie is my daughter. Anything having to do with her is my concern, not yours. It would be best if you remembered that."

He strode off after Kristie, his long, angry strides quickly catching up with her. Ellie stood where she was, abruptly conscious of her wet sneakers and muddy hands. She must look as forlorn as she felt.

Forlorn was definitely the right word. Because as she watched Quinn stalk toward the car without a backward glance, she recognized only too well what was happening to her.

She'd begun to fall for him. Unlikely as it seemed, she'd begun to fall in love with Quinn. And there wasn't the slightest chance in the world that he'd ever feel the same.

Chapter Nine

Ellie took another stitch and then let the doll she was working on drop into her lap. She should be enjoying these quiet moments at the end of the day. Usually she loved snuggling into the rocking chair in her cozy apartment above the shop, rain pattering against the windows, her favorite dulcimer music playing softly in the background. Usually. Not tonight.

How could she relax when her mind kept replaying, over and over again, those moments with Quinn in the meadow? Her every sense had been heightened, and it seemed she still felt it.

She stroked the soft print fabric she'd chosen for the doll's dress, loving the feel of it under her fingers. The trouble with handwork was that it didn't engage her mind, or at least, not enough. Her restless imagination continued to work. It persisted in presenting images of Quinn: of laughing with him, of talking with him, of joining in his family parties and dinners as if she really belonged.

You don't, she lectured herself firmly. *You don't even belong in Bedford Creek. Not really. Not yet. And if anyone finds out about the past...*

That didn't bear thinking about, and she'd worked herself back to the hard lesson she'd learned when a whole town had turned against her. She couldn't risk letting people know the truth. She couldn't face the rejection again. And that meant she couldn't possibly let herself feel anything for Quinn, even if every other obstacle between them disappeared like mist rising from the river on a sunny day.

She'd just reached that dreary conclusion when the back doorbell rang. Hannibal raised his head from the couch, glared at her as if she were to blame for the intrusion on his nap and closed his eyes again.

Putting the handiwork on the arm of her chair, she glanced at the clock. Had her father forgotten his key? No, the movie he'd gone to couldn't possibly be out yet. She shoved her bare feet into moccasins and went quickly down the back stairs.

Two steps from the bottom she could see through

the small glass pane in the door, and her heart gave a little jump. Quinn.

He stood on the other side of her door, rain glistening on the windbreaker that covered his broad shoulders. The porch light touched damp dark hair and shadowed his face.

She opened the door with trepidation, extinguishing an involuntary flicker of pleasure at the sight of him. Had he come to lecture her even further about her relationship with his child?

"Quinn." That didn't sound very welcoming. "What can I do for you?"

"You can let me in." He brushed droplets of water from his hair. "It's wet out here."

She stepped back, making room for him in the miniscule landing at the bottom of the stairs. He stepped inside, bringing the scent of summer rain with him. She moved onto the steps to put a few more inches between them. He always seemed to invade her space, as if he had to take control of every environment.

"Is something wrong?" Her mind flew to Kristie's misadventure.

He shook his head, and a fine spray of rain touched her face. "No, nothing's wrong. I just want to talk with you." He glanced up toward the living quarters. "May I come in? Or if your father's here, we could go somewhere else for coffee."

He didn't sound antagonistic, but she wasn't taking any chances. "If this is about this afternoon, I don't know what else I can say. I'm sorry if you feel I took too much upon myself where Kristie's concerned."

He lifted an eyebrow, his gaze intent on her face. "Are you that reluctant to let me into your home?"

She could hardly tell him to go away, and at some level she didn't want to. "No, of course not." She gestured to the stairs. "Please, come in."

She hurried up, very conscious of his firm footsteps behind her. Her mind raced ahead, doing a quick inventory of how her tiny living room looked. She hadn't expected to have company tonight, and clutter seemed to take it over at every opportunity, no matter how she tried.

"Your father?" he said again, his voice carefully neutral.

"Dad is out. He went to a movie. I was just doing some sewing."

The top of the stairs emerged directly into the living room. She gestured him to a seat, trying to decide how the room looked through his eyes.

Did he appreciate the fine handiwork on the double-wedding ring quilt she'd hung to disguise the stain in the wallpaper over the couch? Would he recognize the effort that had gone into the patchwork cushions, appreciate the deep pink of the cosmos filling the milk glass pitcher? Or would he think it all looked shabby and homemade?

Quinn glanced around, his only reaction a smile at the sight of the sleeping cat. Then his gaze seemed to land on the doll she'd been making. Flustered, she reached for it, intending to stuff it into the workbag that sat next to her chair. But he got to it first.

His hands dwarfed the stuffed doll as he touched the curls made of vermillion embroidery silk. "Is this what I think it is?"

"I'm making it for Kristie's birthday."

He held it for a long moment, stroking the hair, his face unreadable. Then he put it into her outstretched hand.

She took the doll, slipping it carefully into the bag, and straightened again. She had no reason to feel embarrassed that he'd seen it, so why did she?

"She'll love it."

"I hope so. She told me once the only red-haired doll she had was Raggedy Ann, and she didn't know why there weren't any prettier red-haired dolls." She tried to say it lightly, but her throat tightened. It was so poignant.

"Thank you for thinking of it."

She nodded, trying not to imagine she heard caring in his voice. "You wanted to talk about something," she reminded him. She sat in the corner of the couch, leaving the rocker for him.

He turned the chair so that its curved arm touched the couch and sat, planting both feet on the worn carpet. He leaned toward her, face intent, and she braced herself for another lecture.

"I wanted to apologize for this afternoon. I shouldn't have been angry with you, and I didn't have any right to speak the way I did."

She'd been thinking that very thing, but once he said it she couldn't help protesting. "It was my fault. I should have told you."

"Maybe the truth was I was angry with myself." He smiled wryly. "I don't seem to be doing a very good job of meeting my daughter's needs."

His unexpected frankness startled her. "Please— it's all right. You don't have to apologize."

"Yes, I do. My mother told me to." His face relaxed a little, and the hand that had formed a fist on the arm of the chair relaxed, too.

"Seems to me you don't always do what your mother says." She could only be grateful the atmosphere had lightened between them.

"Maybe, but she had a point this time. She said I was overreacting. After all, she hadn't told me, either, and she was the one Kristie confided in."

Some of Ellie's tension seeped away. "I still

think I should have told you. But it was just so awkward.''

Awkward didn't begin to describe it. Her own feelings were all mixed up with Kristie's dreams of a mommy, and talking about this with Quinn wasn't safe. She might let her feelings show.

''Let's just forget the whole thing, all right? Kristie's falling in the creek had already upset us both. Especially when we'd just been looking at the quarry.'' She shivered. ''I know it's beautiful, but it's also dangerous.''

He nodded, mouth tightening again. ''You do know about the accident there?'' He made it a question, not a statement.

''Rebecca told me once about Brett and some friends nearly drowning in the quarry when they were in high school.'' She felt cold, suddenly, in spite of the warm summer night. ''But I didn't think you were one of them, were you?''

''No.'' He clipped off the word. ''That was Brett, Alex Caine and Mitch Donovan. I'm sure you know Alex and Mitch.''

Everyone in town knew them. Alex was the richest man in town, owner of the factory that employed at least half of it, probably. And Mitch, the police chief...

She found she'd tensed, as she seemed to whenever she thought of Mitch. Mitch had never been anything but kind to her, but somehow just the sight of his uniform always reminded her of the secret she hid.

She glanced at Quinn, but his gaze seemed focused on the past. Judging by his expression, the memory wasn't a happy one.

"What happened?" she asked softly.

He shrugged. "They were on our class camping trip when a storm hit. It doesn't take much rain to flood the quarry, and they were trapped. It's a miracle they all got out alive."

Tension seemed to vibrate from him. Odd that it still bothered him after all this time.

"But they did get out." She tried to sound reassuring. "So it's all right."

He didn't seem to hear her. "I was supposed to be in their group that day. But I got out of it. I'd scheduled a college visit, so I left camp early that morning and missed going with them."

"You were lucky," she ventured, hoping she wasn't saying the wrong thing.

"Lucky? People said so at the time." His words were casual, but his hand tightened on the arm of the rocking chair until the knuckles were white. "But if I'd been there, maybe it wouldn't have happened."

"Why would you think that? If you'd been there, you might have been in danger, too."

"They were my friends. I should have been with them." His response was as swift as if it had happened yesterday.

Realization hit her with a certainty she couldn't question. Whether he knew it or not, Quinn might also be talking about his wife's encounter with a drunk driver on a rainy night. The patter of raindrops against the window no longer sounded soothing.

It was the sort of question that always haunted survivors: *Why wasn't I there, why didn't I do something.* How much more it must haunt someone like Quinn, who seemed to have such a need to control everything around him. That quality probably made him a good engineer, but it couldn't be easy to live with.

Her throat tightened until she couldn't speak. Pastor Richie had been wrong about her, she thought. She wasn't the right person to minister to Quinn's grief. She couldn't even get any words out.

"I'm sorry," she said finally. "I know. I guess we always want to be with people we care about when they're in trouble."

Quinn's face was bleak. "Then my record is perfect, isn't it? I've never been there."

The words were barely out of his mouth before Quinn realized what he'd said. He looked at himself, aghast. What was going on here? He'd never said anything like that to anyone, not even to himself. Why on earth had he said it to Ellie, of all people?

She was looking at him with a mixture of sympathy and distress in her dark eyes. She probably didn't know how to respond, for good reason.

"Sorry." That sounded curt, and he cleared his throat. "I didn't mean to get into that."

"Quinn, you shouldn't blame yourself. I'm sure your friends don't."

"Don't they?" He'd never been sure of that, and he'd never felt he could ask them.

"No," she said firmly. "And if you're thinking about Kristie... Well, she knows you love her."

Actually he hadn't been thinking about his daughter. He'd been thinking about Julie, dying on that wet road alone. About his father, battling cancer and not telling him, as if he shouldn't be bothered. He hadn't been there for either of them until it was too late. But he wasn't going to tell Ellie that.

"I know." He shook his head, trying to manage a smile. "You were right—I was upset about Kristie's falling today, especially after we'd just been looking down into that quarry."

"How is she?" She probably wanted to get the conversation back to a more normal level, and he couldn't blame her for that. "No ill effects, I hope."

"None the worse for her ducking." He tried to force a light note into his voice. "We had a talk about her interpretation of scripture. I hope she's beginning to understand she can't play matchmaker for me, but I wouldn't bet on it."

Her smile looked a little strained. That was hardly surprising. "I think I mentioned before how determined she is. We'll have to keep reinforcing the fact that we're just friends."

Friends, he thought. No, he wouldn't say they were friends. They'd started out as adversaries. Then, perhaps, they'd become reluctant allies. But that moment in the meadow—if Kristie hadn't yelled, he knew he'd have kissed her.

Would he? The thought startled him. He hadn't been consciously thinking of that when he came here tonight. But now that it was in his mind, he couldn't seem to think of anything else.

She'd stood there looking up at him with a question in her brown eyes, and the sunlight had kissed her skin and highlighted the rose in her cheeks. And he'd wanted to kiss her.

It had been a trick of the light, he told himself. The scent of wildflowers, the emotions stirred up by a familiar place. That was all. It could have been any other woman in that time and place, and he'd have responded in the same way. He was only human, after all.

Except that there was no sunlight here, only yellow lamplight and the sound of the cat purring. And he was feeling the same thing. He reached across the inches between them to clasp her wrist. Her pulse thundered against his hand. Her gaze met his, and he knew that she was remembering, too.

"This afternoon, if Kristie hadn't fallen just then…"

"Nothing," she said quickly, as if she could read his thoughts. "If she hadn't, nothing would have happened." She seemed to be trying to convince herself.

"Wouldn't it?" He leaned closer. The rain tapped against the windows, and the plaintive sounds of a ballad came softly from the tape player. The yellow cat stretched on the couch and put one white paw over his eyes. He'd never been in a place that felt so much like home. "Seems to me something might have."

"It shouldn't."

He touched her hair, and the glossy strands wove around his fingers as if they were alive. He'd wanted to do that for days, he realized.

"It shouldn't," she said again, but her face tilted toward his.

"I think so," he murmured, and then his mouth

found hers and stilled whatever protest she might make.

She was warm and sweet, and she smelled like the meadow had that afternoon. His palm cradled her soft cheek, and the blood pounded through his veins. He wanted to pull her closer. He wanted to go on kissing her for hours.

She drew back, her lips a whisper from his. "This isn't a good idea."

"Why not?" He felt as if he were continuing an argument he'd already started with himself. "We're both free."

She drew back another inch, and he was sure the movement was reluctant.

"Our parents," she reminded him. "Kristie. It wouldn't be fair to let her think her wish is coming true. Besides, you'll be leaving soon."

Leaving. Longing flickered through him, and he pushed it away. He would be leaving soon, and he didn't intend to walk away from problems when he did.

He stood quickly, before he could give in to the temptation to kiss her again. "You're right. I'll be leaving soon. And I guess that's what I'd better do right now. I'll see you in the morning."

He spun and thudded down the steps before he could give in to the longing to stay.

* * *

Quinn was escaping, Ellie thought as the outside door closed. He already regretted kissing her and just wanted to get away. Certainly she regretted that kiss.

His mouth had been warm and firm against hers. Feelings had tumbled through her, too quick to recognize. They'd swept away rational thought, until the only thing left in the world had been the touch of his lips.

She reached out a shaky hand to stroke the cat. "You should have stopped me, Hannibal. You should have stuck your claws in me before I got anywhere near him."

Hannibal yawned delicately, showing a pink tongue, as if to indicate he didn't believe a word of it. Then he closed his eyes again.

How had this happened? She glanced around the quiet room as if an answer had to be there someplace. She'd spent years being mindful of her secret past, holding it up as a shield against letting anyone get too close. She'd become an expert at rolling into a prickly ball when anyone attempted it.

Until Quinn. How had he gotten past her defenses? She looked back over the last week, but no answer appeared. She'd recognized Quinn for the threat he was, yet somehow he'd managed to touch her heart.

No, not her heart, she protested, panic-stricken.

She might be attracted to him—any normal woman would be. But she couldn't let herself care for him.

She sat very straight, wrapping her arms around herself. That kiss had been a mistake. Quinn undoubtedly realized that just as well as she did. She regretted it, and she'd pretend it hadn't happened.

Liar, a soft voice spoke in her mind. *You don't regret it at all. And you won't forget it.*

Maybe she didn't regret it. Maybe she couldn't deny the feelings that stirred in her. But that didn't mean she had to act on them. Because if she did, the results could sweep away everything she cared about.

Chapter Ten

"It's time to sit down on the story rug now," Ellie announced the next morning. She could only hope she didn't sound as distracted as she felt. Overexcited children, the last day of VBS, the closing program for parents looming—those were all good reasons for her mood. Unfortunately none happened to be the cause.

She tried and failed to keep her gaze from straying to Quinn. He'd settled at the back of the braided rug as he usually did, preferring to let her tell the Bible story. He folded long legs in front of him and leaned back on his hands, strong face as impassive as if it had been carved from redwood.

The muscles in her neck tensed, and she cleared her throat softly. All right, she could get through this. Maybe she did have feelings for Quinn. She'd simply accept that fact and move on. No more fairy-tale dreams for her. She wasn't the princess in the tower, and he wasn't going to ride up and rescue her.

She'd treat Quinn as impersonally as if he were a stranger. She'd be polite, friendly, and she certainly would not dwell on the shape of his mouth or the firm line of his jaw.

And she'd made a fortunate decision, since he apparently felt the same. All morning he'd watched her, but his impassive face hadn't given away a single glimmer of feeling.

So that was it. He'd obviously decided it was best to pretend last night hadn't happened. They were just two strangers forced into a temporary partnership that would soon end.

She opened her Bible, and a shaft of sunlight fell across the final VBS story—Jacob and Esau, and the reconciliation of the estranged brothers. *Forgiveness*. For a moment the words swam on the page.

She blinked the threat of tears away and began the story.

Half an hour later the children clustered at the door, ready to race into Fellowship Hall for their program rehearsal with Pastor Richie. If anyone could settle them down enough to remember their lines and their songs, he could.

"Hey!"

She turned at the sound of Robbie's peremptory challenge, but the boy had fixed his attention on Quinn. Well, good, let Quinn handle it. Maybe Robbie would jolt him out of his silent mode.

"Hey, what?" Quinn looked down at the boy.

"Ms. Ellie says that guy Esau forgave his brother for all those mean tricks."

Quinn nodded, not looking at her. "That's what Ms. Ellie said, so it must be true."

"Well, I wouldn't." Robbie planted his fists on his hips. "If I had a brother and he did that, I wouldn't forgive him, not ever. Would you?"

She waited for Quinn's calm answer, but it didn't come. He looked at the child for a moment, his face grim, then shook his head. "We don't have time to talk about it now. You can ask Ms. Ellie later."

The bell called the children to rehearsal, and they flooded down the hallway. Ellie stood where she was, looking at Quinn. The lines of his face seemed to deepen, as if he were worn down to the bone.

She remembered her intentions to keep things cool and impersonal between them, then pushed them away. She couldn't, not when he looked like that. "Quinn, what's wrong?"

Gray eyes, as hard and impervious as granite, met

hers. "What could be wrong?" He grated the words, his tone denying their meaning.

She wanted to pretend she hadn't asked, pretend she didn't care. *Impossible.* "I heard you with Robbie. You didn't answer his question."

If granite could harden, his expression did just that. "I didn't have time."

She longed to touch him comfortingly, as she would one of the children. Her imagination presented her with the warmth of his skin under her fingertips, and her hands tingled. She pressed her fists into the folds of her full skirt.

"We always have time to answer the children's questions. Why didn't you reassure Robbie about forgiveness?"

Anger flared dangerously in his eyes. "Don't lecture me, Ellie."

"I'm not." She had to steel herself not to take a step back from that bitterness. "I just want to know what's going on. We're teaching together, remember?"

"Not for much longer."

She nodded, conceding the truth. Not much longer. Something inside her wanted to weep at that. "That doesn't change the question, does it?"

His hand moved in a brief, dismissive chop. Then his mouth twisted a little. "Sorry if I didn't pull my weight as a teacher. Maybe you can talk to Robbie about it later. I'm not a good person to ask about forgiveness.''

"But..." She reached toward him before she could tell herself it was unwise.

"Somebody killed my wife, remember?" He threw the words at her. "He got drunk. He got behind the wheel of a car and drove. He killed her. Do you expect me to forgive that?"

His pain seemed to grab her heart and wring it. "It doesn't matter what I expect." She struggled to keep her voice steady.

"You think God expects it, I suppose." His face twisted. "Well, if God thinks I'll forgive that, He's wrong."

He thrust her hand away with a quick, hard movement and charged out the door.

Pastor Richie had worried that Quinn hadn't opened up to anyone since his wife's death. He'd hoped she could minister to him. Ellie wrapped her arms around herself as if that would relieve the pain.

She hadn't ministered to him. The chance had flared up so suddenly she hadn't been prepared. She'd only made matters worse.

And if there had remained a tiny flame of hope in her heart about herself and Quinn, his words had extinguished it. Quinn didn't forgive. He didn't forgive the drunk driver, even though the man was in jail.

He wouldn't forgive her, if he ever learned the truth.

Anger drove Quinn halfway out of the building before he stopped, fists clenched, breathing as if he'd run a marathon. He hadn't let the anger out in a long time. He'd taken pride in controlling himself.

He took another breath. He certainly couldn't say he was under control now. He wanted to go outside, start running up the mountain and keep going until he'd tired out the anger that burned inside him.

He couldn't. Ellie could handle the children without him, but Kristie would be hurt if her daddy weren't there to watch her. He forced his fists to unclench. He'd slip into Fellowship Hall and find a spot at the back from where he could watch his daughter.

With a little luck, no one would bother him, and he wouldn't explode at anyone else the way he had with Ellie. He felt a twinge of regret. Even though she'd pushed him, she hadn't deserved to bear the brunt of his anger.

Parents, grandparents and friends already filled most of the metal folding chairs that had been set up for the program. Amazing, that this number of people could get away from their work at noon on a Friday to watch their children, or even someone else's children, sing a song or two and recite a Bible verse.

But that's how Bedford Creek was. That's how it had always been. If the children were doing something, the whole community turned out to support them, cameras in hand. The tourists would have to fend for themselves for the next hour.

Unfortunately, that same attitude prevented him from successfully disappearing into the woodwork. At least half a dozen people spotted him and stopped to chat—complaints about the wet summer weather, encouraging words about the tomato harvest, smiling approval at how the children had grown.

Had any of that changed in the last thirty years? The conversations sounded exactly the same, but people still felt compelled to make them. That was characteristic of a small town, and he told himself it was annoying. You could never be anonymous and alone. He propped his shoulders against the cement block wall and mutely ordered the program to start.

As if on cue the children filed to their seats. Kristie skipped to hers, her gaze scanning the audience. When she spotted him, her face lit with such pure pleasure that his heart cramped.

How many times had she looked out at an audience and found him missing? He kept telling himself that someday he'd make it up to her, but someday didn't come. How could he go away again? But how could he stay? Bedford Creek brought out the worst in him.

Pastor Richie bounded onto the small stage, consulted his notes, frowned and hurried back off again, to engage in a whispered conversation with several of the teachers. The children buzzed and stirred restlessly. If the pastor and teachers didn't get the program going soon, some of the smaller children would be wandering back to their parents.

"Looks like a glitch in the proceedings." Brett leaned against the wall next to him.

"Looks like," he agreed, wondering what Brett would say if he told him to buzz off. Probably just laugh. It took more than a minor insult to upset Brett. "What are you doing here, brother-in-law? Not enough patients at the clinic?"

Brett grinned. "I think they're all here at the moment. Besides, I had to come and watch my favorite niece, didn't I?"

"Looks as if you're not the only one. Half the town must be here."

Brett nodded toward the audience. "Look at Alex and Mitch down there, ready to beam at their offspring. Pretty soon it will be me. How did we all get old enough to be the grown-ups? I remember when we were the ones performing."

"You were always the one performing," Quinn corrected him. "The rest of us stood reluctantly in the back row of the chorus."

He discovered he was watching Ellie instead of the kids. From her place at the piano she smiled encouragingly at the children, then gave a hushing gesture. They settled back into their seats as if by magic. No matter how guarded Ellie might be with adults, the children walked right into her heart.

Whatever anger he'd been holding against her ebbed away. She hadn't been trying to pry—he knew that. She'd been trying to help. She just hadn't realized what a sore spot she'd touched.

Ellie got up from the piano, exchanged a few words with Pastor Richie and sat back down again. Apparently they were the right words, because the pastor's usual welcome speech got underway.

"Looks as if our Ellie got them straightened out," Brett said. He eyed Quinn speculatively. "She's a pretty woman. Seems like you've been spending a lot of time with her lately."

If that was a question, Quinn didn't intend to answer it. "Pretty, yes. But she's something of a mystery, isn't she? Nobody seems to know much about her past. And whenever anyone gets too close, she curls up into a prickly ball."

"Anyone?" Brett sounded amused. "Or you?"

"I'm trying to protect Mom, remember?" He shouldn't have to remind Brett of that. "Rebecca's the one who thought we had something to worry about."

"Much as I adore her, your sister worries too much." He punched Quinn lightly. "You do, too. Must be a family trait."

"I worry about keeping Charles Wayne away from my mother, if that's what you mean."

Brett shrugged. "He's something of an outsider, I have to give you that. But everyone likes Ellie. And if you're seeing a lot of her...well, why not?"

Rebecca waved, gesturing to an empty seat next to her, and Brett went to join her, leaving his question hanging in the air. *Why not?*

Ellie started down Main Street from the bakery, a still-warm loaf of seven-grain bread tucked into her already-full shopping bag. Bible school had ended successfully, and she actually had a small breather before she launched into final preparations for the craft show. She'd be feeling happy and relieved right now, if it weren't for one thing.

One person, a little voice corrected in her mind.

It was no use. She couldn't stop thinking about that exchange with Quinn in the Sunday school room. Each time she wasn't actively engaged in some other conversation, it started replaying in her head.

She shouldn't have said anything. If she'd just let it go...

But how could she? Pastor Richie was right—they had to try and minister to Quinn. But probably even the wise pastor didn't recognize the depth of Quinn's anger.

And his grief. She frowned, considering that. Of course he must still be grieving, but that wasn't the overwhelming emotion that had rolled at her in waves when she pressed him. Instead she'd sensed anger, vengeance, maybe even guilt. And her questions certainly hadn't helped matters any.

Would she take it back, if she could? She'd had to say something, and possibly anything she'd said at that moment would have had a similar response. Whether Quinn realized it or not, the Bible story that morning had spoken to his soul.

Forgiveness. Thoughts of her father bumped uncomfortably in her mind. Maybe she had issues of forgiveness herself. She'd tried to forgive her father. She'd stood by him, visited him in prison and tried to repay his debts.

But when he'd been released, he'd promptly vanished. For five long years, she hadn't known where he was. She didn't understand it. Probably she never would.

"Ellie?"

She jumped, recognizing the hand on her shoulder even before she recognized the voice. "Quinn. What are you doing here?"

"Running some errands for my mother." He glanced at her packages, lifting an eyebrow. "Looks as if you have an armload. Can I take some of those for you?"

"You don't need to...." But he was already taking the shopping bag from her arm.

She took a breath, trying to still the jumble of feelings that invaded her at the sight of him. She hadn't expected to see him again so soon. But since she had, she owed him something.

"Quinn, I'm sorry for this morning." She rushed the words out, before she lost her nerve. "I shouldn't have said anything."

He shook his head decisively. "Forget it. I don't know why I was so edgy, but it wasn't your fault. Or Robbie's."

"I'm sure it rolled right off his back." She hadn't been able to forget so easily, but he didn't need to know that.

"Just like the directions you gave the kids about not rushing the refreshments line. He nearly knocked Mrs. Rolland off her feet, trying to get to the chocolate cake before anyone else."

"I noticed you intercepted him." By the time the

program was over, Quinn had apparently shaken off his anger. He'd stayed for refreshments, talked to parents and generally behaved as if this week of Bible school had been the time of his life.

"I remember a thing or two about little boys and buffet tables." He gestured with the shopping bag. "Do you have other errands?"

He was behaving too nicely, too normally, and it made her nervous. Whatever else you could say about their relationship, you wouldn't call it nice and normal.

She stopped in front of the print shop. "I have to pick up the posters for the craft show." She reached for her bag. "So if you have something else to do, I'll take that now."

"Not at all." He held the bag out of reach. "I'll help you carry them back to the shop. After all, that's partly my mother's responsibility, too, isn't it?"

"That's not necessary."

"Not necessary, but a pleasure." He held the print shop door for her.

Controlling, she thought, not for the first time. He just couldn't seem to help himself. *Determined.* A spurt of annoyance was quickly followed by a flicker of fear.

If he put that same persistence to work on her

past, he'd find out the truth. And she already knew he wouldn't forgive.

Allen Kramer lounged behind the counter at Kramer's Print Shop. He didn't look up until Ellie stood directly in front of him. "Ellie. Is there something I can do for you?"

"I'd like to pick up my poster order."

Kramer's eyebrows rose. "Poster order? You don't have a poster order with us."

"Don't have... What are you talking about?" She felt a wave of panic. "I talked to you ages ago about doing the posters for the craft fair. I sent my father up Monday with the design. They were supposed to be done today."

Kramer had started shaking his head at her first words, and he just went on shaking it. "Nope."

"What do you mean?" She herself felt like doing a little shaking of him. Kramer was always casual about deadlines, which probably came of being the only print shop in town. "I have to have those posters. The committee expects to put them up soon."

"Better talk to your father about that." Kramer drew himself up, clearly offended. "Came in here with that design and questioned my price. Said it was too high. So I said he could just take his business somewhere else, and off he went."

She couldn't let him see how disturbed she was.

Even worse, she couldn't let Quinn see. She managed a smile.

"I guess we got our wires crossed, then." She probably should apologize, but the man was so smug she couldn't bring herself to do it. "I'll check with him about it."

Dad, what have you done now? I trusted you, I gave you the money.... Her heart twisted. Was that what this was about? The money?

She made it out of the shop, very conscious of Quinn on her heels. She turned to him, wanting nothing more than to be rid of him. She held out her hand for the bag. "It looks as if I don't have to pick those up after all. I'd better get back to the shop now."

The frown Quinn directed at her made it clear he wasn't going to accept her dismissal. "What's going on with the posters? Why didn't you know what your father did?"

She tried not to let her dismay show in her face. "I'm sure it's just a misunderstanding. I'll see Dad and straighten it out."

She grasped the shopping bag. He let her take it, then closed his hand over hers so that they stood locked. "Level with me, Ellie. I can see you're upset. Why?"

"If I'm upset, it's because you're making a

mountain out of a molehill.'' She tugged at her hand. ''People are watching us.''

He glanced around, apparently realized that was true, and dropped her hand. ''You looked like your worst nightmare had come true when Kramer told you what your father had done. If this affects the committee's work, my mother has a right to know.''

''But you don't.'' She turned anger at her father into anger at him. ''You're hoping this will make my father look bad, aren't you?''

His face hardened. ''Sounds to me as if he's done that all by himself.''

She wanted to argue, wanted to say he didn't know her father, but she couldn't. Maybe she didn't know him all that well herself now.

But one thing she did know. She knew that the brief truce between her and Quinn had just been broken.

Chapter Eleven

Ellie shoved the shop door open so hard that the bell nearly jangled off its hook. She didn't know if she was angrier with Quinn or with her father. She just knew that it flared inside her like a physical pain. And beneath the anger was the thing she didn't want to recognize—fear.

"Ellie, what's wrong?" Her father stood behind the counter, looking as comfortable there as he once had in his corner office. "You look ready to bite someone." His smile held an edge of concern.

"I guess I am." Thank goodness the shop was empty of customers. "I just stopped at the print shop for my posters, but they weren't ready. Because you never gave them the order."

"Well, no." He flushed. "I was going to tell you about it."

"Dad, how could you? You know I need them to advertise the craft show! I'll never be able to get them in time now."

"Ellie, it's not what you think."

"Well, what is it, Dad?" She dropped her packages on the counter. "You tell me. This craft show is important. It's my way of repaying people here for their kindness. I trusted you to take care of ordering the posters, and you let me down."

She stopped abruptly, astonished that the words had actually come out of her mouth. *You let me down.*

It was what she'd always thought, always felt, and never said to him. She hadn't said it even in the worst of times, when the newspapers trumpeted his name and people avoided her on the street.

Her father, who never showed his age, suddenly looked very old. Shaking his head, he reached for something beneath the counter.

"I let you down once, Princess, in the worst way possible. I won't do that again." He lifted an unwieldy stack to the countertop. "Here they are."

Ellie took a step forward and pulled the brown paper covering aside. The craft fair posters stared up at her, their colors bright and appealing, looking even better than she'd expected.

"I don't understand." She touched them, as if to be sure they were real. "Where did these come from? Kramer told me he didn't do them, and his is the only print shop in town.''

"I suppose that's why he thinks he can over-charge." Her father's voice regained a little brisk-ness. "I went to Henderson instead. Gwen lent me her car. They did them while I waited."

"You went all that way? Why didn't you tell me?''

"I wanted to surprise you." His smile was crooked. "I guess we were both surprised."

"Dad, I'm sorry." She didn't know what to say.

He shook his head and pulled a pale blue rectan-gle from his pocket. "Here's your check back. The posters are my gift to the craft fair."

She stared at it blankly. "You don't have to do that. I'm sorry."

"You thought I let you down." Tears glistened suddenly in his eyes. "It's all right, Ellie. I don't blame you. After all, that's what I did before. You have every right to be angry with me for that."

"It's not that. It's… You went away." The words burst out before she could stop them. "You got out of prison and just disappeared." She sounded like a lost child, crying for her parent. "How could you do that to me?''

"Oh, Ellie." He came around the counter to her. "I'm sorry. I was just so ashamed. You'd started a new life, and I didn't want to interfere with that.

Besides, I had a debt to repay. I guess my pride got in the way. I didn't want to come back to you until I'd repaid every cent I'd taken—until I felt forgiven.''

"You repaid..." She couldn't take it in. "All this time I thought..."

"You thought I didn't take responsibility for what I'd done." He took both her hands in his, and she felt him tremble. "Maybe I didn't for a long time. But God kept working on me, until He brought me to my knees. I believe He's forgiven me. Now I'm asking you. Please forgive me, Ellie."

Something seemed to break inside her, and her tears spilled over. She stepped forward into her father's arms.

"Please can't I have just one taste of icing? Please, please, please?"

Laughing, Quinn disentangled his daughter's arms from around his legs. "Don't you think your guests will notice if there's a great big Kristie fingerprint in the middle of the cake?"

She tipped her head, considering that, then spun around. "Maybe Grammy has some left in the icing bowl." She ran toward the kitchen.

He started to follow, but the doorbell rang. He glanced at his watch. Guests arriving already. Kristie's birthday party was getting underway, and she'd have the cake soon enough.

He swung the door open, and the welcoming smile seemed to freeze on his face. Ellie and her father stood there, side by side, both holding packages. Given the way he and Ellie had parted the day before, he wouldn't have been surprised if she'd made an excuse not to come.

Her smile looked about as stiff as Quinn's, but Charles greeted him as if they were long-lost brothers. "Quinn, what a perfect evening for a birthday party. Where's the birthday girl?"

"In the kitchen, trying to con some extra icing out of her grandmother."

"No, now she's run outside to pick a few more mums for the table." His mother hurried in from the kitchen and enveloped Ellie in a hug. "She's so excited you'd think she'd never had a birthday before. I just hope she's not still thinking—"

"Of course not." He interrupted before his mother could blurt out anything potentially embarrassing. "We got that all settled." At least he hoped so.

"Perhaps you'd like to put our package with the other presents." Ellie handed him a box wrapped in pink, and his fingers brushed hers as he took it.

They both knew what was in the box. The memory of the night he'd seen the doll danced in his mind. Unfortunately it wasn't the thought of the doll that made his heart beat a little faster.

When Kristie had announced she'd wanted to invite Ellie and her father to her birthday party, his feelings had been mixed, to say the least. Maybe the truth was he'd like to have Ellie here, without Charles.

She snatched her hand away, the warm color in her cheeks deepening. Pointedly ignoring him, she turned to Gwen and held out the flat package her father had been holding.

"Here are the craft show posters you said you'd put around town. I've already taken them to the stores down at my end of River Street."

"Wonderful." His mother smiled. "I'll take them around on Monday, once this party is off my mind." She looked at Ellie's father. "Charles, would you like to help me bring out the plates?"

Charles shot a wary glance at Quinn, then followed her toward the kitchen.

Ellie made a move as if to go after them, but Quinn caught her hand. He wanted some answers before she disappeared. "I take it the poster snafu worked out all right?"

"It was a misunderstanding." She fired the words at him. "I told you that. My father got a better deal on the posters over in Henderson."

That couldn't be all of it, or she wouldn't have

looked the way she had in the print shop. "He just forgot to tell you about it?" He lifted his eyebrows, knowing they were both thinking of those moments and her anger.

Her mouth firmed, as if denying him access to whatever it was she thought. "He wanted to surprise me. That's all. There weren't any problems."

"I'm glad."

"Are you?" It was a challenge.

"Yes." The truth of it astonished him. "I'm glad everything's okay."

They stood motionless for a moment, his hand clasped around hers. He had the sense of things unsaid passing between them—the sense that words trembled on her tongue, wanting to be said.

Then the doorbell rang again, and Kristie raced in to answer it. He let go of Ellie reluctantly and turned to greet the arriving guests, wondering what they might have said to each other, given the chance.

The party swirled around him for the next hour. Kristie had invited a mixture of family and friends that somewhat surprised him. Brett and Rebecca, of course, but also Alex, his fiancée, Paula, and his son, Jason. Maybe that was understandable, because Jason was only a year or so older than Kristie. Even Robbie was there.

But she'd also asked Mitch and Anne Donovan.

Their foster son was a gangling adolescent, and little Emilie, the toddler, he'd think was too young to play with Kristie.

Family and friends, he thought again, watching Kristie find a balloon for Emilie. Kristie had created a party from the people who meant the most to her, including Ellie and Charles. How did they fit in?

Surprisingly well, he decided, watching them. No, he might as well admit the truth, if only to himself. Watching her. He couldn't stop watching her.

Something had changed between Ellie and her father, he could sense it. Some tension that had existed before was gone.

She glanced up, and her eyes met his as if she felt his speculation from across the room. Those dark, thick lashes swept down again, hiding her eyes, but she couldn't hide from him. They understood each other. He didn't know how or why, but they saw into each other without the need for words.

He turned away, confusion flooding through him. This couldn't be. What he was thinking was just plain crazy. He took a step or two and paused by the piano.

A photograph of his father sat on top of the piano, in the center, surrounded by pictures of him and his sisters at various stages of life. John Forrester looked out of the silver frame with the grave smile that had been so characteristic of him.

"I miss him, too." His mother's voice startled him. "Every day."

He put his arm around her soft shoulders. "I know. It doesn't seem fair that he can't be here to celebrate with us."

She patted his hand. "In a way, I think he is. I guess I need the comfort of feeling that."

He couldn't stop his gaze from straying toward Charles. She nodded, seeming to understand what he didn't say.

"I know. You don't like my seeing Charles. But it doesn't mean I'm forgetting your father. It just means that I need someone to share things with. Can't you understand that and be happy I've found someone?"

"I would be." He tried to believe that. "If I were sure you'd found the right someone."

"Isn't that my decision, dear?" Her voice was very gentle.

She turned and hurried off toward the kitchen before he could find an answer. Maybe he wouldn't have found one very quickly in any event.

He looked at Ellie again. She was organizing a game of Pin the Tail on the Donkey, laughing as she tied a blindfold on Brett. If he were able to let go of his suspicions of her father, if he could accept his mother's judgment and leave it at all, where did that leave him with Ellie?

"Goodbye, goodbye, goodbye!" Ellie watched as Kristie waved to her aunt and uncle, then spun and ran to the back porch. She crawled up onto the swing next to Ellie, hugging the new doll tightly.

"I just love her." She leaned against Ellie's arm. "Did I tell you that?"

She stroked the child's hair. "About a hundred times." She glanced at Quinn, who was tidying up the grill where he'd fixed hot dogs and burgers for supper. "You could probably tell your daddy again how much you love your new bike."

Quinn looked up, smiling, a lock of his usually neat dark hair falling onto his forehead. "I think she already did that."

Kristie had ridden the new bicycle up and down the driveway time after time, until she could do it with no help at all. The triumph on her face when she'd gone all the way on her own had been worth seeing. Quinn had to know how much she enjoyed her gift.

Did he also know how much Ellie had enjoyed the evening? The tension that usually disrupted the time she spent with Quinn had been absent, even when her father was near. It almost seemed that Quinn had accepted their part in his mother's life.

No, that was too much to hope for. Quinn had just been on his best behavior because all of his friends were at the party. And since everyone else had left, they should go, too.

"I think we'll say good-night now." She hugged Kristie. "I'm glad you like your doll."

"Amelia," Kristie corrected. "I'm going to call her Amelia." Her face clouded. "You can't go now."

Quinn came onto the porch, wiping his hands on a towel. He tossed it over the railing. "It's starting to get dark, honey. Time for you to get ready for bed."

"No, no." Kristie shook her head firmly. "Not yet. Charles promised to tell me a story about San Francisco." She slid off the swing. "I'll go find him, okay? He can tell me the story, and then it will be bedtime." She scurried into the house, the doll tucked under her arm.

Ellie expected Quinn to intercede and waited for him to object. Instead he shrugged.

"Have you noticed how often she outmaneuvers me?"

"It had occurred to me."

He sat down in the place Kristie had vacated on the swing, seeming in no hurry to put his daughter to bed. The wooden swing creaked under his weight, and he pushed gently with his foot. They swung back and forth, the creak a soft counterpoint to the crickets in the hedge. Fireflies began to rise from the grass, painting swirls of light against the deepening shadows.

Quinn's face was in profile to her, and she realized she was studying the crisp strong lines as if she needed to memorize them. Her nerves seemed to be standing at attention, as if every cell in her body was aware of him, sitting so close. She should leave, but she couldn't seem to make herself get up.

"You surprised me." She said the words without thinking.

He turned to her, raising straight, level brows. "How so?"

"Do you really want my father telling her stories? Isn't that a change?"

"I don't suppose a story or two will do any harm." The corners of his mouth quirked slightly. "Seems to me you're the one who's changed toward him."

She felt as if the porch floor had just tilted, leaving her stumbling for balance. "I don't know what you mean."

"Just what I said. Every time I've seen the two of you together, I've noticed a strain. Until tonight. Tonight, things are different."

"You're imagining it." Surely he couldn't see

into her feelings that much. If he could, she was in more trouble than she'd thought.

"I don't think so. What's changed between you? Does it have something to do with the posters?"

She leaned back against the arm of the swing to give herself another inch or two between them. The wooden arm pressed, unyielding, into her back. "You like to ask questions so much maybe you should have been a lawyer instead of an engineer."

"Lawyers have to stay indoors too much. I couldn't handle that. I just like to know how things work. And people."

"You must have been the kind of child who's always taking things apart."

His slow smile made her heart turn over. "How else could I know what made them work?"

Keep it light, she ordered herself. *Don't let him see the effect he has on you.* "I'll bet your parents really enjoyed that."

"Mom got frustrated, I have to admit. Especially when I dismantled the toaster on the day she was having her church circle in for brunch." He shook his head, then casually stretched his arm along the back of the swing. It pressed against her shoulders. "I'll bet she's thankful every day that Kristie doesn't take after me in that respect."

"I suppose." She clasped her hands together in her lap, sure they were giving away the tension she felt at his nearness. "Kristie's like you in a lot of other ways, though. I'm sure your mother enjoys that."

"I hope so." He frowned. "I hope it's not getting to be too much for her."

She didn't know what to say to that. Gwen adored her granddaughter and loved having her here. But Gwen and Kristie both longed to have Quinn home for good.

He glanced at her, his eyes questioning. "No opinion on that?"

"My opinion doesn't matter," she said carefully. "It's how you and Gwen and Kristie feel about it that's important."

"Yes, I guess it is. And it was time I came home and figured that out." He turned his body to face her, and his hand curved over her shoulder. "You know, I seem to owe your father a vote of thanks."

"For what?" If she weren't so distracted by the strength of his arm and the warmth of his hand, she might be able to come up with an intelligent response.

"If I hadn't been worried about his relationship with my mother, I might not have come home when I did."

"You don't have to worry…" she began, but the words became trapped, then lost, when he touched her cheek. Her skin tingled under his fingers, and her breath caught.

"And if I hadn't come home when I did, I wouldn't have gotten to know you." His voice grew husky, and he leaned closer. "I wouldn't want to miss that."

She couldn't speak, couldn't think, couldn't even breathe. All she could do was lift her mouth to his.

His hand slid into her hair as his lips found hers, and his arm tightened around her, drawing her close against him. She couldn't have pulled away if she'd wanted to, and she didn't want to. Her arms went around him, touching the strong, flat muscles of his back.

She was where she wanted to be, and she never wanted this moment to end.

Chapter Twelve

Ellie found herself singing as she wiped down the counter in the shop on Monday morning. She tried telling herself she was singing praises because God had given this lovely day, but that was only part of the truth. The rest of the reason was both more complicated and more selfish—Quinn.

Silly, wasn't it? She looked out the window at what she could see of Bedford Creek. The maples in the park across the street waved in the light breeze, and sunlight glinted on the river. Beauty did surround her, but Quinn filled her mind.

He'd let down his guard with her. He'd kissed her. For a few minutes she'd felt closer to him than she'd ever felt to anyone in her life. Surely she wouldn't feel that way if something weren't meant to be between them.

But the barriers hadn't disappeared just because Quinn had kissed her. Even though she'd resolved the strain between herself and her father, that didn't change history, however much she might want it to.

Her father had embezzled, he'd been caught, he'd been sent to prison. Charles honestly believed that wouldn't make a difference in how Bedford Creek viewed her. He was wrong. She'd lived through that revelation before, and she knew.

Nothing had changed. She had absolutely no reason to be so happy. But she sang another chorus of "Bringing in the Sheaves" while she swept the wide wooden floorboards.

The bell above the shop door jingled. She stood, dustpan in her hand, and tried to control the joy that flooded her.

"Quinn, I didn't expect to see you this morning." But she'd hoped.

He stood motionless just inside the door, a silhouette with the light behind him. Then he moved, and she saw no answering smile. Without speaking, he flipped the sign to Closed and turned the lock.

Something chilled inside her. "What are you doing? Why…"

His grim expression dried up her words. He took a step toward her. "Why? Because I don't think either of us wants the conversation we're about to have interrupted."

Something was wrong, very wrong. She tried to swallow the apprehensive lump in her throat. "What is it? What's happened?"

He glanced toward the expanse of glass across the front of the shop. A pair of early tourists looked at the sign, then peered through the window. "Maybe we'd better go upstairs."

Mutely she nodded. She turned and forced herself to walk up the steps, feeling as if she were mounting a scaffold.

What was it? Her mind darted from one possibility to another. Something about Kristie, something about her father? Had Charles done something else to upset Quinn?

She emerged into the living room. The sunlight that had brought joy moments before now only seemed to make the room look shabby. She turned to face him.

"What's happened?"

The lines in his face deepened, and his granite stare turned implacable. "You lied to me." He threw the words at her like four separate stones.

"I don't know what you're talking about." She tried to keep her voice calm while her mind twisted and turned. "When did I lie to you?"

His right hand made a short, chopping motion. "Don't play games with me, Ellie. I know the truth.

The private investigator I hired found out everything there is to know about you and your father.''

''Private investigator?'' For an instant sheer anger swamped every other emotion. ''You hired someone to investigate me? How could you?''

His mouth twisted in what might have been a smile, except that it held nothing but mockery. ''Funny, that's the question I started asking myself last night. How could I investigate Ellie, the person everyone loves? How could I be so suspicious? So I phoned the firm this morning, intending to call them off. But they already had a report for me. Shall I tell you what it said?''

Something inside her seemed to shrivel up and die. She didn't need to worry any longer about telling him the truth, did she?

''I suppose it said that my father had a prison record.'' It took all her strength to keep standing upright, looking at him.

''You suppose right.'' His body was stiff with anger. ''A prison record for embezzlement—for stealing from his employer. And you brought him to Bedford Creek, introduced him to people who had befriended you and never said a word of warning.''

She took a breath, trying to suppress the tears that threatened to clog her voice. Be angry. It was much better to be angry with him. That way she could hold the pain at bay for another moment or two.

"My father's past is no one's business. Should I have taken out an ad in the paper, announcing his failures? Or maybe you think he should wear a sign."

"Failures?" His eyes flashed. "Crime, Ellie. Call it what it is. Embezzlement is a crime."

"Yes, it's a crime." She threw the word back at him. "I'm sure your private investigator filled you in on all the details. But did he tell you my father spent the last five years working to repay every single cent? My father has changed, whether you believe it or not."

If that mattered to him, it didn't show. "What I believe isn't important, but the truth is. My mother is supposed to be your friend, yet you let her become involved with him and didn't tell her. What kind of a friend hides a secret like that?"

"I care about Gwen." She turned away from him, suddenly too exhausted to keep on fighting. "But I couldn't tell her. I couldn't tell anyone."

"So you lied."

Her fury came raging back at his contemptuous tone. She swung on him. "Lied? I tried very hard never to lie to anyone, but I certainly didn't volunteer anything. I knew what would happen when people found out. I've been there before—believe me, I know.''

''What are you—''

''You don't know.'' She swept on, carried on a wave of pain. ''You don't know because you've always belonged. You can't begin to imagine what it's like when everyone you care about turns against you. And now it's going to happen all over again.''

She turned away, fighting back tears. He had to get out of there, now, before she broke down completely in front of him.

''Ellie...''

''Please, just go away.'' Her voice broke on the final word, and she took a shaky breath that ended in a sob. ''It's over.''

Her pain reached out and wrapped itself around Quinn's heart. He didn't want it to cut through his anger and touch him. He didn't want to, but he couldn't help it.

''Ellie...'' He said her name again, his voice tight. Before he could think about it, he grasped her shoulders and felt the anguish that wracked her. He turned her toward him and pulled her into his arms.

''Don't, Ellie.'' He murmured her name into her hair. ''Don't hurt so much.''

He wasn't sure she heard him. Sobs shook her, and he felt hot, wet tears against his shirt. He didn't know whether to blame her father or blame himself. All he seemed able to do was hold her.

"Shh." He stroked her back as he would Kristie's. "It's going to be all right." He murmured soothing words, not sure she was hearing him, not sure he even meant them. This wasn't going to be all right. How could it be? But he couldn't stand the pain she was in.

Finally the sobs lessened. She took a long, shuddering breath and pushed away from him.

He let her go reluctantly. But she clearly wouldn't want him to comfort her, not if she could help it. She wiped her eyes with the back of her hands, as a child would.

"I'm sorry."

"Don't be." He had to find a way to deal with this. He took her arm, leading her to the couch, and sat down next to her. "I was angry. I came here intending to hurt you." He looked at that truth bleakly. "I just didn't realize how much you were already hurting."

She took a breath, interrupted by a small sob. "Everything you said was true."

"Yes." Everything he'd said had been true, but he'd had a choice about what he did with it. He'd used it to strike out at her, and that didn't exactly make him proud of himself. "Tell me, Ellie. Tell me what happened."

She shrugged, then wrapped her arms around herself as if cold. "You already know, don't you?"

"Facts, that's all. I don't know how it hit you." He took her hand. It felt like ice. "You couldn't have been very old when he was arrested."

For a moment he thought she wouldn't respond, but then she seemed to force out a word. "Eighteen."

He swallowed. When he was eighteen, he'd felt as if he had the world at his feet. "How did you find out?"

"We were at a dinner at the country club, with all our friends, my father's business associates." Her hands twisted convulsively in his. "I didn't have any idea that anything was wrong, until the police came in and arrested him."

She stopped, as if that was the end of the story. His imagination presented him with the picture, unrolling in front of him as if he'd been there. A younger Ellie, vulnerable and innocent, lost when the father she loved turned out to be a criminal.

"You must have had someone to help you—family, friends."

She shook her head, pulling her hand away from his. "No one. We didn't have any other family. And when it came out, the people I'd thought were our friends acted as if he'd cheated them personally." Her mouth firmed. "That wasn't surprising,

I guess. His employer owned the mill that supported the whole town. He was like a little king. No one would go against him to support an embezzler.''

''You didn't do it. They couldn't blame you.'' He wanted her to say it wasn't so. To say she'd had friends, people to support her. He didn't know why it was important, but it was.

She started to shake her head and just went on shaking it. ''I was tarred with the same brush as my father. That's how it was. That's how it will be again, when people here know.'' Her face grew bleak. ''I'll have to leave.''

An hour ago, he'd have welcomed those words. But then he'd been blind with anger. He'd told himself that anger was for his mother's sake, but it wasn't. Truth was, he'd been furious because he felt betrayed.

He'd begun to care for Ellie. He'd never intended to. He didn't know how it had happened. But he had, and the knowledge that she'd deceived him cut through his pride to his heart.

''People here aren't like that.'' He'd like to believe that. ''No one will turn against you because of what your father did.''

She looked at him as if they came from different planets. ''Why not? You did.''

He wanted to deny it, but there was too much truth in what she said. He'd been suspicious of

Charles from the beginning, and that had inevitably colored everything he said and did.

"All right, maybe you have a point. Maybe, if people knew you hadn't been honest with them about your father, it would change how they look at you. But they're not going to know about it from me."

Her startled gaze flew to his face. "Not?"

"What did you think, that I'd start a whispering campaign about you? Of course I'm not going to blab it around town."

Something that might have been hope began to dawn in her eyes. Quickly, before she could say anything, he went on.

"But there's one person who has to be told. My mother."

"You haven't told her?"

"It should come from you." *You're her friend.* But he wasn't going to beat her with that anymore. She'd taken enough from the father who'd betrayed her and the so-called friends who'd let her face it alone. Anger seared along his nerves.

She took a breath, seeming to call on some reserves of strength deep inside. "All right. When?"

He stood. "Now."

Not sure her legs would support her, Ellie forced herself to her feet. She made herself take a breath, then another. How could she possibly keep going when it hurt so much? She pressed her fist against her diaphragm, trying to control the pain, and started down the stairs. Quinn's footsteps thumped out a dirge behind her.

She'd lost. She'd lost the battle to keep her secret, and she'd lost him.

The thought drove the pain deeper. *No.* She couldn't lose something she'd never had, and she'd never really had Quinn's love. Maybe, if things had been different for both of them, it might have been possible. But it wasn't.

Quinn held his car door for her, and she got in. She tried to put a glass barrier between them as he drove. If she could just keep her heart walled off from him, maybe she could get through the ordeal of telling Gwen.

A fresh wave of pain assaulted her. Gwen's face, angry as Quinn's had been, formed in her mind. She'd deceived Gwen. How could she possibly forgive that? And once Gwen knew the truth, how long would it be before everyone in town knew?

Panic fluttered at the thought of what would follow. She couldn't—she couldn't go through that again.

Maybe Gwen wouldn't tell. The thought formed in her mind, and she clung to it. Maybe, if she understood why Ellie had kept her secret, Gwen wouldn't tell. That might be the only hope she could salvage from this disaster.

By the time they reached the house, that faint hope was all that kept her going. Then Quinn opened the side door and stepped into the kitchen, and they relived the past all over again. Gwen and her father sat at the kitchen table together.

Quinn's fists clenched, and anger rolled off him in waves. "What are you doing here?"

"Quinn!" Gwen's feathers ruffled. "I won't have you talk to my friend that way."

"Gwen, please." Ellie forced the words out past the lump in her throat that threatened to choke her. "Dad, I think you'd better leave."

In an instant he'd reached her side. He put his arm around her, drawing her away from Quinn. "Princess, what is it? What's wrong?"

"Dad, just go home." She tried to detach herself. "It's better."

"Maybe he should stay." Quinn grated the words, all the anger back in his voice. "This is about him. Go ahead, Ellie. Say it."

She leaned against her father's arm for a moment. "I'm sorry, Dad." She looked at Gwen. "There's something I have to tell you about myself. About my father."

"Ellie, honey…" Her father hugged her. "You don't need to."

"Yes, I do." Didn't he understand that it was over? Couldn't he see that Quinn knew? "I have to."

"No, you don't." Gwen's voice took command. "You don't have to tell me, because I already know. I know all about Charles's conviction and his prison term. I've known for days."

Ellie could only stare. Gwen's soft, round face hadn't changed. Her hands still fluttered. But determination shone in her eyes. "You know? How do you know?"

Gwen looked at Charles, and her expression softened. "Charles told me himself."

Her father stroked her hair. "Honey, I know you didn't want me to tell anyone here about the past. But when Gwen and I became friends, I couldn't keep it from her. That wouldn't have been fair."

Fair. She was the one who hadn't been fair, either to Gwen or her father. He'd had the courage she didn't.

Lord, how am I going to get through this? What can I possibly say?

"Ellie, it's all right." Gwen patted her hand. "I haven't told anyone, and I won't." She looked at Quinn. "And neither will Quinn."

Quinn looked as if he'd been hit with a brick. "He told you?" He focused on his mother. "Mom, I appreciate the fact that he leveled with you, but that doesn't change anything. He still committed a crime.''

"And he paid for that. He went to prison, and when he got out, he worked until he'd repaid every single cent." Her gaze softened as she looked at her son. "You have to let me make my own decisions, Quinn. I'm not a child, and I don't need to be protected."

"Dad..." Pain crossed Quinn's face as he said the word.

"I know." Gwen reached for his hands. "It was always so important to him to take care of me. So I let him." She focused on him, face intent. "But I don't need you to step into his shoes. I can take care of myself. Can't you let me do that?"

Ellie could see the struggle in him so clearly, even though none of it showed in his face. How had that happened? Her heart hurt even more. How had she become so close to him that she could see into his heart?

Finally he nodded. "All right, Mom. If that's what you want, I won't stand in your way."

"And you won't tell anyone, will you?" She clutched his hands for emphasis. "That's what Ellie wants, and we have to respect that."

His face tightened as he looked at her. "I've already told Ellie that."

"Thank you." Her lips were almost too stiff to form the words. "Dad, I think we'd better go."

He didn't argue. His arm around her, he piloted her to the door. He didn't speak until they were safely outside. "Princess, I'm sorry." Tears filled his voice. "I've hurt you again. I'm sorry."

She leaned against him. "It's all right. You did the right thing, telling Gwen."

"She won't say anything." She felt the hesitation in him, as if he weighed saying something more. "But Ellie, don't you think you should?"

"I can't." Surely he realized that. "I don't want to lose people I care about." *Anyone else I care about.*

"Honey, I know. Don't you think I've been there?"

What was he saying? "I don't understand what you mean."

He held her close. "Princess, I got into trouble because I tried to live a lie to impress people, and the only way to maintain that lie was to take money that didn't belong to me. I just don't want you to make the same mistake I did."

"It's not the same."

"In a way, it is," he insisted. "If you love these people, you have to stop living a lie. Don't you think their love is strong enough that you can trust them with the truth?"

Chapter Thirteen

Two days. It had been two days since the truth had come out, and she hadn't seen Quinn in all that time.

Just the thought of him was enough to send her heart into spasms of pain. Surely it wasn't possible for a heart to hurt this much and keep on beating, but it did.

She sought for something good to cling to—her renewed relationship with her father, the strength of her faith. Those would carry her through.

At least Quinn had apparently kept his word. He hadn't told her secret.

Ellie ducked under the portico sheltering the church door and folded her umbrella, shaking it. The rain had been relentless all day. She could only hope enough of her volunteers had braved the weather to work on the booths for the craft fair. And if she could concentrate on that, maybe she could stop thinking about Quinn.

She hurried inside to find Fellowship Hall abuzz with activity. People scurried back and forth, carrying boxes of craft items, arguing over jobs, hammering together the wooden booths they'd hoped to set up on the church lawn. Then all of the action seemed to freeze, and she saw only one person.

Quinn stood, a hammer in his hand, in the shell of a booth. Mitch held out a board to him. Quinn didn't take it. He didn't move. His gaze fixed on her, his expression unreadable. Then the moment broke. He turned away, taking the board, making some comment to Mitch, and everything flowed on.

She pressed her hand against her rib cage, feeling as if he'd hit her. But what else could she expect? She'd deceived him. To his way of thinking, she'd betrayed him. Maybe he'd felt reluctant sympathy when he'd seen the depth of her pain, but that was all.

"Ms. Ellie, Ms. Ellie!" Kristie skipped over, her red hair as wiry in the damp weather as if it was spiked with electricity. "I'm helping with the craft show. Grammy said I could."

"That's wonderful, Kristie."

The child's voice had drawn other people's attention to her, and she was immediately besieged with questions about the fair. Pastor Richie hurried over, waving them off.

"All right, all right, we'll make a decision. Just give us a moment." He smiled at Ellie and shook his head. "Everyone has an opinion, of course. What do you think? You're the committee chair. Can we have the fair outside, the way we planned?"

"Ask me an easy question." She grimaced. "The weather forecast says the storm is going to move off the coast by tonight, but do we want to count on that? Gwen, what do you think?"

Gwen handed the sign she was making to Charles. "I'm just not sure. What if the forecast is wrong? Then what?"

What if Quinn saw his mother and her father together? She reminded herself she didn't have to worry about that any longer. The truth was out between them now. In a way, it made things so much easier.

For a brief moment the thought of letting the whole town know about her father's history flickered through her mind. Her father would be all right with that. Even Gwen would.

She was the only one not brave enough to risk it. She hadn't even been brave enough to pray for guidance, afraid of what that guidance might be.

She forced herself to concentrate on the discussion.

"The problem is, if we wait, we might not have time to finish all of the booths." Pastor Richie frowned. "But if we finish them in here, we won't be able to get them through the doors to take them outside." He shook his head. "There's no good answer."

They were all looking to her for a solution. She took a breath. *Think about the job at hand. Don't think about Quinn. Don't wonder if he's listening or what he's thinking.*

"I say we'd better commit to having the fair in Fellowship Hall. I know it's not what we planned, but I don't want to take the chance of ruining it entirely. Okay?"

Pastor Richie nodded. "That's what I like. Someone who's not afraid to make a decision. Okay, everyone, let's get this done. We're going with inside."

Not afraid to make a decision? She wanted to laugh. If he only knew the truth.

For some reason the story she'd told the children about Abraham popped into her mind. She heard again Kristie's question. *But wasn't Abraham scared to go off on a long journey just because God told him to?*

She'd told the children Abraham trusted God

enough to do what God wanted. That had been easy to say, but it wasn't so easy to do. Here she stood, afraid even to take her problem to God—afraid to hear His answer, let alone trust it.

Pastor Richie nipped his thumb with a hammer. "Ouch." His eyes twinkled. "I'm not sure carpentry is my strong suit."

She took the hammer from him. "We could probably find you something safer to do."

He shook his head. "I want to help." He glanced toward Gwen and Charles. "Your father seems very handy with tools. Was that what he did before he retired?"

The innocent question hung in the air. Ellie tried to breathe—tried not to let the thought into her mind. But it came anyway.

She could evade the question. Or she could let the truth come out. She could, like Abraham, trust the Lord.

The words pressed on her lips as if they wanted to be said. She took a breath, reaching out in prayer.

I'm stepping into deep water here, Lord. Please don't let me drown.

She opened her mouth, not sure what was going to come out. "My father was assigned to the carpentry shop for several years while he was in prison for embezzlement. He says it was the only positive thing about the experience."

The words came as easily as if she'd been talking about the rain. No one would guess the leap of faith they represented.

She heard a startled gasp somewhere behind her and knew what it meant. Her long-held secret would be all over the room in minutes. She forced herself to meet Pastor Richie's eyes.

She discovered nothing but sympathy there. "I didn't know."

"I've hidden it for a long time." She felt an odd sense of release at admitting it.

He patted her shoulder. "Secrets can be heavy burdens. You have to use up a lot of energy keeping them from escaping. Maybe it's better this way."

Some of the tension she'd been carrying for days slid away. Maybe it *was* better, although she couldn't expect other people to take her revelation as calmly as Pastor Richie did. He took everything calmly, as if he'd seen it all. Still, for better or worse, it was out.

Thank you, Lord. Now please, help me deal with the fallout.

She straightened, looking around the room, feeling the murmurs spread from person to person. Her gaze tangled with Quinn's. Her heart gave a momentary leap of totally irrational hope, and then she quashed it.

Quinn stared back at her, totally expressionless.

He wouldn't care that she'd finally exposed her past. It was too late now.

For a moment Quinn didn't believe his ears. He blinked. Just like that, after all the secrets and lies, Ellie had told.

"Whew." Mitch spoke softly. "That's quite a little bombshell from our Ellie."

"Isn't it, though?" He tried to sound noncommittal.

But Mitch had known him too long. His dark eyes surveyed him, and Quinn realized that his friend the cop was somewhat like Pastor Richie. He saw things other people didn't.

"You already knew," Mitch said.

Quinn shrugged, pounding a two-by-four into place. "I did some investigating into Charles Wayne's past. After all, Charles has become quite a friend of my mother."

"I see." Mitch glanced across the room. "Looks like your mother isn't bothered by his record."

"No." He clipped the word and slammed the hammer with unnecessary force. It didn't help.

"Guess this explains something that always puzzled me about Ellie." Mitch grinned. "She's never really warmed up to me. Not that I'm the most lovable guy in the world, but still…"

"Yeah, right." Quinn found himself smiling

back, feeling again like the kid he'd once been, kidding around with his friend. "That's why you ended up married to the smartest, most beautiful lawyer Bedford Creek has ever seen."

"That was luck," Mitch said. He glanced at Ellie and sobered. "Ellie will need a little luck, I'd say. Some people won't take this as well as Pastor Richie."

"I guess not." The words pricked him like a nettle. That wasn't his problem, Quinn told himself. Ellie had brought this trouble on herself.

It took a lot of courage to come out with it, a small voice remarked in his mind. *She's already suffered enough for something that wasn't her fault.*

Ellie wasn't his problem. But he couldn't keep from watching her, even as he turned back to his work. He couldn't help wondering what she was feeling. What had made her blurt it out, after all this time? Did she already regret it?

His mother moved to Ellie's side, murmured something in her ear, then gave her a quick hug, exuding strength and compassion.

Had his mother really changed? Or had that strength been there all along, and he'd just never seen it? Maybe he'd been guilty of looking at her simply as his mother, instead of as a person with a mind of her own and the will to use it.

His mother had moved off, and another woman paused by Ellie. Next to him, Mitch straightened.

"Uh-oh," he said.

"What?"

Mitch raised his eyebrows. "Don't you recognize Enid Lawrence? You've been away too long, buddy, if you were able to forget her. That woman has the bitterest verbal attack in three states. I should know. She's turned it on me often enough."

"I'd forgotten. My dad used to say she'd curdle milk just by looking at it."

He couldn't hear what Enid said to Ellie. But he could guess at the content. Ellie's expressive face went white, and then as scarlet as if she'd been struck.

He was still telling himself it wasn't his concern when he was halfway across the room. By the time he got there, Enid had said a word or two to Charles and gone on her poisonous way.

Quinn stopped in front of Ellie, searching for words. He didn't know what to say, and he hadn't realized Mitch was behind him until his friend spoke.

"Let me give you a hand with that, Charles." Mitch lifted the end of the board Charles held. "I'll help you get it up."

Charles shot him a thankful look, nodding. Something, maybe a sense of relief, ran through the room. Quinn could almost feel what people were thinking. If the police chief accepted the man, he couldn't be too bad.

Ellie's dark eyes filled with gratitude, and Quinn had to suppress a spurt of jealousy. He could hardly expect her to look at him that way.

"Are you all right?" he said in an undertone, not especially wanting to advertise his concern to the whole town.

Her expression turned wary. "I'm fine."

He reached for the stack of boxes she held. "Let me help you with those."

She pivoted, setting them down, her back stiff. "I don't need any help."

A spurt of anger—or was it hurt?—flared at her quick dismissal. He didn't want to look too closely. "So you're grateful to someone who helps your father, but you reject anyone who tries to help you."

Her cool stare seemed to put him at a distance, as if she was looking at him through a telescope. "I don't need your pity, Quinn."

"I'm not…" What could he say? That he didn't feel sorry for her? She'd know it wasn't true, and she'd reject that, too.

She was still looking at him as if he were the guilty party. His jaw clenched. The truth was, he couldn't tell her what he felt because he just plain didn't know. And that was a pitiful admission to make.

A few drops of water, left from the all-day rain, pattered from the trees in the park onto Ellie's hair as she walked that evening. She tilted her face back, enjoying their cooling.

This had been one of the longest days of her life. She had desperately needed a few minutes alone, and the rain and the drawing in of evening had emptied the park.

She paused under the lifted branches of a river birch and glanced back at Bedford Creek. *Her town,* she thought as she had so often over the last few years.

Was it? She loved it here, but was it really her place now that the truth was out? She still wasn't sure.

As for Quinn... She turned and walked swiftly toward the river, as if she could outrun her thoughts. She didn't want to think about Quinn, because that hurt too much.

The split-rail fence that guarded the riverbank felt wet and smooth under her hands. She leaned against it, trying to concentrate on the gray water, trying not to think it was the same color as Quinn's eyes.

That was a useless exercise. She couldn't stop

thinking of him, and it was foolish even to try. Maybe, after he'd gone away again, the pain would lessen. At least then she wouldn't have to be constantly keyed-up, expecting to see him around every corner.

"A little wet out for a walk, isn't it?"

She hadn't heard Quinn's approach across the wet grass, and she spun around to face him, heart pounding. He wore the shuttered expression that told her nothing of what he thought or felt.

"What are you doing here?" She hugged herself, suddenly chilled through the light windbreaker she wore.

He stopped next to her, leaning his side against the fence as he looked down at her. "I came to see you. Your father told me where you were."

She turned toward the river again, planting her hands on the wet rail. It was much easier to look at the high water than to look at him and wonder what he was thinking. "I'm surprised you're speaking to my father."

She felt, rather than saw, his shrug. "Charles isn't a person to hold a grudge, is he? He greeted me like a long-lost friend." Quinn turned, putting his elbows on the fence next to her, looking out at the river as she did. "He's worried about you."

His arm brushed hers, and she had to stifle the impulse to spring back as if she'd received a shock.

Be careful, she warned her fragile heart. *Don't start imagining he cares about you. He feels sorry for you, that's all.*

"No one needs to worry about me." She tried to sound as if she believed that. "I'm fine."

"Are you? This can't have been an easy day."

That sounded like genuine concern in his low voice, and she tried to hold up a barrier against it. If she let his concern in, believing it was real, she might crumble. She'd done that once with Quinn, humiliating herself by crying her heart out. She wouldn't do it again.

"I didn't expect this to be easy." No, not easy. *But the worst part is you, Quinn. Don't you know that?*

"How did people behave the rest of the day?"

Her cheeks went hot at the memory of Enid's barbed comments. "Luckily everyone isn't as bitter as Enid." She shrugged. "Some people were all right, others hostile. Some were just cool, as if they reserved judgment."

"I'm sorry."

"Don't be." To her surprise, she meant it. She wouldn't blame him for this. "Actually, it wasn't as bad as I expected. As I remembered. Maybe because it's old news, or maybe because I'm a little more mature now than I was at eighteen."

"Maybe you're stronger than you know." His

arm pressed against hers, sending a thousand messages along her nerves that she tried not to heed.

"Pastor Richie said a secret is a heavy burden. It feels good not to be carrying it any longer, no matter what happens." She forced herself to look up at him. "So I guess I have to thank you."

He lifted his dark brows, and his eyes gleamed with what might have been humor. "Is that comment sarcastic, by any chance?"

"No." Some of the tension she carried slipped away. "I mean it. If you hadn't forced the issue, I might not have found the courage to let it out."

His hand closed warmly over hers. "I'm still sorry for the way I went about it."

"But not for doing it." She shook her head quickly, before he could speak. "That wasn't a criticism, really. You wanted to protect your mother. I understand that."

"You wanted to protect your father."

"And myself," she admitted.

His fingers tightened around hers, and she felt their warmth all the way up her arm. "There's nothing wrong with that," he said softly.

She tried to think through the jumble of feelings roused by his nearness. Was he saying he was able to forgive? Had she actually made a dent in that implacable nature of his?

"I don't..." She lost whatever she was about to

say in his intent gaze. He was so close that her emotions welled up, catching her by surprise. She wanted… She wasn't sure what she wanted.

Liar, her heart retorted sternly. *You want to be in his arms.*

His eyes darkened suddenly, like a storm moving up the river. "Ellie." His voice roughened on her name.

She shook her head, not sure what she tried to convey. Her lips parted, but no words came out.

He released her hand, and for an instant she felt cold and lost. Then he touched her face, hands slipping under her hair, thumbs brushing her cheeks. Emotion filled her—need, longing, tenderness.

He was so close, so close. Then his mouth claimed hers, and the world spun off in a dizzying spiral. She heard the rush of water from the river, and it seemed to be sweeping her away to a world where only she and Quinn existed.

He drew away for an instant, brushing kisses against her cheek, the corner of her mouth. "Ellie." He murmured her name against her lips.

Be careful, she tried to tell herself, but it was no use. She couldn't possibly be careful where Quinn was concerned. She couldn't guard her heart. She could only hold him close and know she loved him.

Chapter Fourteen

"**W**here does this go, Ellie?"

Ellie decided she must have answered that question fourteen times in the last hour, but the craft fair was finally shaping up. She glanced around the church hall the next morning with a sense of satisfaction.

Fewer volunteers had shown up this morning than the day before, but she wouldn't let herself speculate on whether that was due to yesterday's revelations or today's even wetter weather. Only one absence really bothered her—Quinn hadn't come yet.

Just the thought of his name brought a warm glow to the heart she'd assumed was broken for good. When they'd stood locked in each other's arms by the river, she'd felt more cherished than she ever had in her life. Maybe she even felt loved.

The feeling went to her head, banishing the sober cautions she probably should heed. She didn't care about that. She didn't want to be cautious, or careful, or have to guard her heart from pain. She wanted to shout her love aloud for everyone to hear.

Instead she went sedately across the room to where Gwen was arranging a display of crocheted pot holders in one of the craft stands. Kristie had been helping her grandmother a moment ago, but now she chased Jason Caine around and around the funnel cake stand.

She could ask Gwen where Quinn was, couldn't she? There was nothing wrong with that.

"That looks nice." She admired the rainbow array of pot holders Gwen had hooked onto a sheet of Peg-Board. "Are all of those from Isabel Strong?"

Gwen nodded, smiling. "She can't see too well now, poor old dear, but she says her fingers still know how to make pot holders, since they've been doing it for nearly ninety years."

"At that price, everyone who comes through the door should buy at least one." She touched a pink knit baby bonnet lightly, hoping her voice wouldn't change. "By the way, I noticed Quinn isn't here. Do you know if he's coming?"

"Oh, I'm sure he is, dear." Gwen's eyes twinkled. "He wouldn't miss helping, I know. But he had a phone call just as we were leaving. It must have been business of some sort."

Business? He surely wasn't going to cut his leave short, was he? Her heart sank. "What made you think it was business?"

"He just looked so serious, I thought it must be." Gwen squeezed her hand. "I'm sure Quinn will be here any minute now. He knows we're expecting his help today. Don't you worry."

She considered protesting that she wasn't worried, but decided it would just draw more attention to her feelings for Quinn. *Her love for Quinn,* she corrected. She might at least be honest in her thoughts.

Was it possible Quinn had said something to Gwen the night before about his feelings? No, Gwen's knowing look probably had nothing to do with that.

"I'll catch up with him later," she said, and went quickly off to check on the soft drink machine.

She'd just convinced the soft drink vendor to cut his prices in view of the charitable nature of the fair when she heard the creak of the door opening. She glanced up to see Quinn's tall figure framed in the opening.

While she was still considering the advisability

of going to him, his gaze swept the room and settled on her. He indicated the outside with a jerk of his head and held the door invitingly.

Trying not to hurry, she crossed to him. Quinn caught her arm in a firm grip and hustled her outside.

"It's a little wet out here, isn't it?" She repeated his remark from the night before, but he didn't smile in response. The gray rain streaked down relentlessly. They stood in the shelter of the portico, close against the church building. "Looks as if the weatherman was wrong again."

He didn't answer, and his grim expression sent a chill down her spine. "What is it?" She caught his hands in hers. "Quinn, what's wrong?"

"I had a call this morning."

"You don't have to go back to Oregon to the project, do you?" She probably sounded as plaintive as Kristie would. How could he go away again when they'd just begun?

"The project?" He looked startled for a moment, as if he'd forgotten about that. "No, it's not that." His mouth tightened, lines bracketing it.

No, not the project. This was obviously something much worse. Tension jerked up a notch inside her. "What is it, then?"

"The call was from the prosecutor's office." At her blank look, a muscle jumped in the hard line of his jaw. "The ones who prosecuted the driver who killed Julie."

"Why were they calling you now?" She'd assumed that was over and done with long ago.

"They wanted me to know the driver is up for parole. It looks as if he may be released early."

She wasn't sure how to respond to that. Quinn had obviously been glad the man was in jail, but she hadn't thought beyond that.

He didn't seem to expect a response. He gripped her hands until they hurt. "I can't let that happen."

"Quinn…"

"I can't," he snapped. "He killed Julie."

Her heart cramped. He'd loved Julie that much— so much, the thought of the driver's release tied him in knots. Maybe he still loved her, loved her too much to give himself to someone else.

She tried to put her own pain aside long enough to deal with his. "What can you do? It's not up to you."

Quinn, can't you let it go? Can't you forgive? But she already knew the answer to that one. He couldn't.

"That's where you're wrong." He wore his need for vengeance like a mask. "Family members can testify at the parole hearing. I'm going. By the time I get done with him, he'll be lucky to get out in twenty years."

She stroked his hand the way she'd comfort a child. "Quinn, I know how much you must miss Julie, how wonderful your marriage must have been."

She had to force the words around the lump in her throat. She couldn't expect he'd ever feel that way about her.

"Wonderful?" For the first time he seemed to look past his anger and focus on her as if he really saw her. His mouth twisted. "I don't suppose Julie thought it was too wonderful. If she had, maybe she and Kristie would have come with me on the job. But she didn't want to change her life, didn't want to move to a new place or have new experiences. The lure of being with me wasn't enough to change that."

She tried to adjust her image of their marriage. Apparently it hadn't been the perfection she'd imagined. "I'm sorry. But you...you can't change the past by seeking revenge."

Did he even want revenge, in his innermost heart? Or was he trying to assuage the guilt he felt for what his marriage hadn't been?

"Justice," he snapped, pulling away from her. "Not revenge, justice. Look, I have to leave. I'm sorry I won't be here to help with the fair. Tell my mother for me, will you? And Kristie."

The wind whipped a spray of water across her

face like tears. He was going. "Aren't you going to say goodbye to them?"

"I have to leave now," he repeated. "If I tell her, Mom will try to talk me out of going, and I'll be lucky to make it in time for the hearing as it is. I just wanted you to know."

"Why?" She caught his hand as he turned away, preparing to run back out into the steady rain. "Why me, Quinn?" She had to know that, at least.

She read the struggle for an answer on his face. "Because I want to know you'll be waiting for me when I come back." He blurted the words out as if almost afraid to say them. "Look, I don't know where this is going between us." He gripped her forearms. "I don't know. But I want... I guess I want to know you're with me."

Her heart gave a leap of hope, and then turned to lead. What he was really saying was that he expected her to approve of what he was doing. And she couldn't—she couldn't. If he wasn't able to forgive and put the past behind him, he could never be whole again.

The temptation to say nothing sang sweetly in her ear. *Just let him go,* it whispered. *You're not his conscience. Let him believe you approve, and save what you have with him.*

No. If she'd learned anything from the situation with her father, it was that only honesty would do between people who loved each other. But if she were honest with Quinn now, she'd lose him.

You'll lose him anyway, her heart responded. *He can't love you when he's caught up in the need for revenge. Either way, you lose.*

Quinn shifted impatiently, waiting for her answer, not sure why it was so important to him. He had to get on the road, but somehow he hadn't been able to go without seeing Ellie. The pressure to leave was a physical drive inside him, surging along his nerves.

"Quinn, can't you let it go?" Ellie's dark eyes were huge and troubled. "This isn't going to do any good for anyone."

"I have a responsibility. Don't you see that?" Why couldn't she understand?

"Your responsibility is to your mother and your child now, not to Julie. I can't believe she would have wanted you to seek revenge for her death." She clutched his hands, her eyes pleading with him.

He pushed her hands away, rejecting the words, anger riding him. "You barely knew Julie. You don't know what she would want. Besides, I owe it to her."

"Why?"

She wouldn't leave it alone. He couldn't think why he'd believed she would understand.

Because I let Julie down. Because whatever it was she wanted, I couldn't provide it.

She'd been so sweet, so young, when they'd met, with a touching willingness to rely on his every word, unlike Ellie, with her determined questions. It was only after they were married that he realized Julie wasn't going to grow any stronger.

"Why, Quinn?" Ellie repeated.

"I just do, that's all. I thought I could count on your support."

Her mouth trembled for an instant, then firmed. "I can't tell you to do something I think is wrong."

He struck out with the only weapon at hand. "You weren't all that righteous when you lied to everyone about your father."

Pain flickered across her face, shaming him. He wanted to take it back, wanted to make things right with her, but he couldn't. The anger he'd been carrying around for nearly two years burned along his veins.

She lifted her chin, looking at him steadily. "All I can say is that I've learned from that. You have to forgive before you can accept forgiveness. Living your life in search of revenge isn't right, any more than living a lie is. You're only going to hurt yourself and the people who love you."

She didn't understand. He'd been a fool to think she would.

"Then I guess I'll have to learn to live with that." He turned and ran through the rain to his car.

Pain was a huge, angry knot inside her chest, so big it threatened to suffocate her. Ellie watched Quinn's car turn, then spin out of the parking lot, spraying gravel. He turned up the mountain road and vanished into the gray mist.

She tried to swallow, but her throat was choked with tears that echoed the pelting rain. Tears she couldn't let fall. Whatever might have been between them, it was gone now. She'd had a chance at his love, and she'd turned it away. She wouldn't have a chance again.

She pressed her hand against her mouth, willing back the tears. She didn't have time to grieve now. People depended upon her, and she had a job to do.

Father, are You going to make something good come of this? I confess I can't see how, but I'll try to trust anyway.

She took a steadying breath, then another. When she thought she'd conquered the tears, she pushed the door open and went inside.

"Ellie?" Gwen came hurrying to her. "I thought I saw Quinn with you. Where is he?"

"He left." She pressed the pain down again. Obviously she'd have to keep doing that. "He asked me to tell you he had to go."

"Go? Where?" Gwen's voice rose. "I don't understand."

Ellie glanced around to be sure no one was within earshot. "He found out that the driver who was in the accident with Julie is up for an early release. He's going to the hearing to try and prevent that."

Quick tears filled Gwen's eyes. "Oh, dear. Why did this have to happen now, of all times?"

She blinked back her own tears. "I don't know."

"He seemed to be doing so well. I really thought he was letting go of his bitterness, especially since…" She stopped.

"Since what?"

"Well, since you, dear." Gwen patted her hand. "I thought you were good for him."

"I wish that were true." Oh, how she wished it. "I tried to convince him not to go, but I'm afraid I just made things worse."

Gwen blotted the tears that escaped onto her cheeks. "It's not your fault, Ellie. I've prayed and prayed Quinn would come home so we could help him get rid of his bitterness. When I finally got him to come, I thought everything would work out all right."

"You got him to come," Ellie echoed, wondering. "Gwen, did you use your relationship with my father to goad Quinn into coming home?"

"Of course not!" Gwen's cheeks went pink with indignation. "Well, only a little bit. I mean, when I saw that it upset Quinn, I decided that was a good thing. It did bring him home, didn't it?"

She wouldn't have thought Gwen could be so devious. "Wasn't that a little unfair to my father?"

Gwen flushed a bit deeper. "Oh, Ellie, I do care for Charles on his own account, you know."

"I know." She squeezed her friend's hand. "He's a lucky man to have you care about him."

Gwen sighed. "I confess, I thought Kristie's prayers were finally going to be answered. I thought she was right—that you were the one God picked out for Quinn."

She felt as if she were bleeding inside. "I guess God must have something else in mind."

She tried to say it lightly, but Gwen must have heard the pain underneath, because she wrapped her arms around her. Ellie leaned her head on Gwen's shoulder, trying to hold back the tears that wanted to overflow.

The door swished open behind her, and she swung around. Quinn... Hope blossomed in her heart, to be quickly trampled. It wasn't Quinn, it was Mitch.

Bulky in his police slicker, Mitch glanced around the room as if he couldn't believe his eyes. "What are all of you doing still here?"

"What do you mean?" Ellie asked. The room slowly became quiet.

"You haven't heard the radio?"

She shook her head, feeling bad news coming.

Mitch's face was grim. "This storm's not going anywhere. It's stuck right over us, and they're saying now we'll get a good ten inches of rain before it's done. The weather service has issued a warning—river's going to crest well above twenty feet. We're in for a flood, folks."

For a moment silence greeted his words. Then a clamor of questions and exclamations burst out. Ellie's mind raced. Twenty feet—she'd lived through a couple of minor floods since she'd come to Bedford Creek, but nothing anywhere near that. The shop...

"Ellie, I expect you want to get down to the shop and start taking stuff to the second floor." Mitch was briskly efficient. "Maybe Gwen can keep a crew here to be sure everything's up on tables."

Ellie nodded, her mind starting to function again. The church was high enough to be safe from the river, but even here, ground water could cover the floor.

Mitch raised his voice above the babble. "Anybody who's able to had better report to sandbagging detail. We'll meet down by the bridge. We've got to get organized quickly. Looks like the flood is going to be a bad one.''

Heart pounding, Ellie grabbed her jacket and hurried out into the rain. It slanted into her face as she ran to the car.

Flood, she thought again, the word echoing in her mind. They were going to have a flood, and Quinn was out somewhere on the road on his mission of revenge.

Lord, protect him, please. Bring him back to us. She stood for an instant, staring at the road he'd taken. *Please, Quinn, come back. Please.*

Chapter Fifteen

Rain pounded against the windshield so fiercely that the wipers couldn't keep up with it. Quinn leaned forward, peering through the murky grayness that was barely pierced by his headlights, trying to make out the lines on the two-lane back road that led to the interstate. Anyone would think it was midnight instead of early afternoon.

He glanced at the clock on the dash. Time was running out. If he didn't arrive at the courthouse by four, his chance to speak at the hearing would disappear. Anger burned along his veins.

Did the prosecutor even care if that happened? Why hadn't they let him know sooner about the parole hearing? When he'd fired that question at the person who'd called, the answer had been evasive.

She'd claimed some sort of bureaucratic mix-up, but he didn't quite buy it.

Maybe the truth was that no one cared—no one but him. Julie hadn't had anyone else to care. The man who'd taken her life with his carelessness had served less than two years, and people had already forgotten. The prosecutor's office had moved on to other cases. Friends and family told him to forgive and forget. *Ellie* told him to forgive and forget.

No, that wasn't fair. He saw again the caring and pain in her face as she talked. Ellie hadn't looked for an easy answer. She wanted what was best for him. They'd just never agree on what that was.

He tried to find some feeling inside, but there was only numbness when he thought of her. Maybe that was best. He didn't seem to have anything to offer that she wanted.

A truck roared past him, going the other way too fast on the narrow mountain road, and sent a torrent of muddy water sluicing across his windshield. The car swerved, and he struggled with the wheel to right it, heart suddenly pounding.

Ridiculous. He'd driven in much worse than this. Why was he letting it affect him?

Then he knew why. Julie had been out on a road like this, on a night like this—wind whipping the rain, branches slashing, the pavement glittering like black ice. She must have seen the headlights coming toward her on the wrong side of the road. She wouldn't have known what to do. She'd have panicked.

Stop it, he ordered. *Thinking like that does no good at all.*

Ellie wanted him to forgive. He saw her face again, dark eyes pleading with him, the mellow stone of the church behind her. He'd wanted to pull her into his arms and bury his face in her hair. He'd wanted to hold her forever.

But she didn't understand. How could she expect him to forgive?

She forgave, a voice whispered in his mind. *Her father destroyed her whole life, and she forgave.*

He grappled unwillingly with the thought. He wanted to believe Ellie didn't know how he felt, but he couldn't. She'd been where he was, and she'd forgiven. She looked into the darkness in his heart, and she still loved him.

Love? He looked at the word cautiously. It hadn't been said between them. How could he believe that was what she felt?

Red taillights ahead of him signaled a warning. He pumped the brakes, sliding a little, and came to a stop behind a lineup of cars on the narrow road. A figure in a black slicker battled through the rain toward him, and he rolled down his window.

"What's happening?"

"Mudslide on the road ahead." The state trooper wiped his wet face with a wetter hand. "They're trying to clear it now. Shouldn't be too long."

The need to move surged through him. Time was ticking away, and any delay could mean he wouldn't get there in time. "Any other way I can get onto the interstate headed east?"

The trooper looked at him as if he'd lost his mind. "East? Haven't you been listening to the radio? The interstate's closed going east. The governor's declared a state of emergency for ten counties. We're dealing with a major flood."

The man turned to wave down a car behind Quinn's, and Quinn snapped the button on the radio, apprehension clutching his throat. He listened to the news, and a slow, sick feeling spread through him. Creeks and rivers were rising at an alarming rate. Flooding was inevitable, maybe as bad locally as the Agnes flood of '72. Bedford Creek sat right in the path of it.

Kristie, his mother…Ellie. *They* were right in the path of it.

"We're right in the path of it." Mitch Donovan stood just inside the shop door, shaking water from his slicker. "The good news is that the rain's slacking off a little upstream. It looks as if the river will crest some time overnight."

"And the bad news?" She feared she knew what it was.

"Bad news is, the crest is going to be well above flood stage."

A low murmur greeted his words, but no one stopped working. They weren't surprised. Ellie had turned the radio on as soon as she reached the shop, so they'd listened as they worked. Local stations had stopped playing music to air a steady stream of flood-related news.

Mitch looked around the shop, seeming to weigh what remained to be done. "Do you have enough help? I'm afraid I can't spare anyone else right now."

"We're fine," she assured him.

She gestured toward the people packing wreaths and candles into boxes and carrying them upstairs. Some had come with her from the church. Others had simply appeared and started working, not waiting for directions.

"We'll have it all on the second floor within the hour." She managed a smile. "I don't even know all these people, but they're helping."

"Nothing like an emergency to bring out the best in people." Mitch glanced at Enid Lawrence, who was folding quilts and putting them in plastic bags. She was also complaining in a querulous voice about the ineptitude of emergency management and flood control, but she worked while she complained. "Even some surprising people."

Ellie nodded. She'd stopped being surprised an hour ago. Now she was just thankful. She wouldn't let herself think beyond that.

"As soon as we're done here, I'll be out to join the sandbagging."

"Good." Mitch shoved the door open and flashed her a smile. "We'll get through this, never fear. We've been through worse."

Her father slid his arm around her waist. "Are you all right, Princess?"

She glanced around at the denuded shelves, wondering if she'd ever see the shop that she loved back to normal again. She shook off the fear and gave him a quick hug. "I'm fine, Daddy. I'm glad you're here."

He blinked rapidly, as if to hold back tears. Then he straightened his shoulders. "Well, now, let's get the rest of these things moved. By the time the water comes, we won't leave anything here for it to ruin."

She had her father back. No matter what else happened, she had him back. *Thank you, Lord.* She tried not to think about the person she didn't have back, but it was useless. *Why couldn't I help Quinn, Lord? Even if a relationship between us wasn't meant to be, even if he could never love me, why couldn't I help him?*

The question echoed in her mind while she cleared the store, sandbagged the doors, thanked the friends and strangers who helped. It continued to reverberate in the back of her mind an hour later, when she joined the sandbagging crew by the bridge.

She surveyed the line of sandbags marking off the lowest, most vulnerable sections of the bank. They looked small and helpless. And the river—

Her breath caught. She'd been so busy, she hadn't had time to look. Now she did, and she couldn't look away.

The clear water had turned a muddy brown. Swollen, sullen, it rolled relentlessly, carrying branches, crates and fragments of what had probably been someone's shed. A picnic table floated past, to shatter into matchsticks against the bridge pilings.

Could they possibly stop something that powerful? She seemed to hear the prayer Pastor Richie had said earlier. The Israelites must have thought it was equally hopeless when they'd faced the sea with an army at their back. Encouraged, she went to the pile of sandbags to start carrying.

She soon found herself working in tandem with

the pastor, carrying bags as quickly as they could be filled.

"Do you think this is going to work?" She lugged a sandbag into place, starting the second layer.

Pastor Richie straightened, hand on his back. "Maybe. I hope so." He shook his head, and water streamed from his hat. "All we can do is our best, Ellie. Beyond that, we have to leave it in God's hands. Do you remember the lines from the Song of Songs? 'Many waters cannot quench love; rivers cannot wash it away.' I find that a comforting thought right now."

Many waters cannot quench love. Her heart contracted.

Quinn, where are you? Are you safe? Why aren't you here with the people who love you?

Quinn pounded the steering wheel in frustration, staring blindly out at the row of stationary cars washed by the rain. Where were the people he loved? Were they all right? Were they taking precautions?

His mind presented him with a terrifying image—a wall of water sweeping down the valley, carrying everything in front of it. He'd seen that once, in a canyon in Colorado. He knew the implacable nature of a flood confined in a narrow valley. He knew the devastation it could bring.

He forced his engineer's mind to zero in on flood-control measures upriver from Bedford Creek, trying to assess how well they'd work. Piecemeal. They were always piecemeal. No matter how the professionals tried to stress the importance of the whole area cooperating, it didn't happen. No one knew what effect the floodwall at Barclay would have on the towns downriver—towns like Bedford Creek.

If the rain kept falling, if the wall held in Barclay, forcing the river into a narrower channel—if, if, if. This could be worse than the flood in '72, when the whole lower end of town had water up to the second floor. Ellie's shop, across from the park, had no protection.

She'd have moved things to the second floor by this time, wouldn't she? He imagined her struggling to save her shop, putting herself in danger, and pain wrapped itself around his heart. He should be there. Instead he was stuck here while people he loved faced danger without him.

Like always, the soft voice of his conscience commented. *That's what you did before, isn't it? You let the people you loved face danger without you.*

His friends, facing death in the flooded quarry;

his wife, facing death on a rain-swept road—he hadn't been there.

God, what have I done? For the first time in too long he cried out to God. *I thought I'd find peace by punishing the person who drove the car that killed Julie. But I'm the guilty one. I'm the one who wasn't there. I'm the one who needs forgiveness.*

His hands clenched the wheel so tightly, its ridges seemed to burn into his palms. Ellie had known. She'd seen it, when she'd told him he was hurting himself by not forgiving. He couldn't have God's forgiveness for himself if he didn't forgive others.

Hot tears stung his eyes. He'd been clutching his need for revenge too long. It had become a part of him, and it was hard to let go. But he had to, or he'd never be whole again.

Help me, Father. Forgive me, and help me forgive.

Someone tapped on the window. He took a breath, searching for calm, and opened the window.

The state trooper stood there. "They've got the road clear now, sir. You can get through, if that's what you want."

"No." Peace filled him as he said the word. "I don't need to go forward. I just have to go back. I have to go back home."

Chapter Sixteen

❧

How much longer could they keep going?

As long as they had to. Ellie tried to steel herself. They didn't have a choice. Maybe a cup of coffee would help, she thought as she dragged herself toward the makeshift food stand that had been set up in front of the police station.

At least the rain had slacked off to a thin drizzle. That had to be good news, didn't it?

Then she looked back at the river and knew it might be too late to make a difference. Sullen and heavy, it rolled inexorably over the park. The pavilion roofs poked above mud-colored water like tiny green islands.

Despair washed over her. Half an hour ago the water had not yet reached the top of the support poles. Now it was well over. The river was still going up. The worst wasn't over.

"Ellie, dear, you need something hot to drink." Gwen, behind the folding table that had been set up under a tarp, forced a plastic cup of coffee into her hand.

"Have you heard anything from…"

Gwen bit her lip, her blue eyes filling with anxiety. "Quinn hasn't called, not yet. But I'm sure he's trying to get back."

"I'm sure he is." Ellie's throat tightened at the thought. Quinn, trying to get back, probably blaming himself again for not being with the people he loved in a crisis. Did he even begin to realize how much his anger was driven by his own sense of guilt? Could he ever let that go?

"Have a piece of apple cake." Gwen forced the paper plate on her, obviously driven by her need to feed people when trouble loomed. "This was baked for the craft fair, but I didn't think you'd mind if I used it."

"Of course not." Her notion of repaying people for their kindness by putting on the fair paled into insignificance when they were all fighting for survival. "The fair isn't important now."

Gwen nodded. "Funny how your priorities change, isn't it? If only I knew Quinn was safe, I wouldn't ask for anything more."

A cold hand clutched her heart, but she managed to smile reassuringly at Gwen. "I'm sure he's fine. He's probably just stuck somewhere. So many of the bridges washed out on the back roads, it'll be hard to get home. But he'll be here—you'll see."

Gwen brightened, as if Ellie's words had helped, and she turned to urge coffee on another weary worker. Now if Ellie could just believe them herself—

Of course I believe. Lord, please keep him safe. Bring him back to us.

She downed the rest of the coffee and headed back to the sandbags.

An hour later it was nearly full dark. Circles of light from rigged-up spotlights played across the scene, turning it into something from an old movie. *A horror movie,* Ellie thought numbly, trying to lug a sandbag that had become inexplicably heavy. Was this never going to end? No matter how many bags they piled up, the water kept rising.

A trickle of muddy water snaked across the road like an advance warning. If the river got much higher, the makeshift floodwall couldn't possibly hold. The water would pour across the road, smash into the buildings—

She stumbled, and a strong hand grabbed her arm.

"What are you doing?" Quinn's voice was

rough with emotion. "You're exhausted. Let me have that."

"I'm fine." She snatched at the sandbag, then realized how ridiculous she must sound, fighting over a sandbag. "You're back."

She looked up at him, feeling as if she'd never get enough of looking. He was back, safe and sound. Shadows darkened his eyes, and worry had etched lines in his face. But he was back.

"Took me too long. I should have been here hours ago." He looked around at the nightmare scene. "My mother? Kristie?"

"They're fine," she said quickly. "Gwen's helping with the canteen over by the police station, and Kristie is with your sister up at the clinic. She's taking care of Hannibal for me, so that's keeping her occupied. Brett's running the first-aid station here."

"Good. I got trapped behind a mudslide and never even made it to the interstate."

So he hadn't made it to the hearing. He'd come back because he had to. Nothing had changed, except that this time he wouldn't have to blame himself for not being here.

"Look, Ellie, I have to talk to you, but I've got to go and help Mitch. Go find something safer to do, will you please? If the water breaks through, I don't want you here."

Before she could argue, he kissed her quickly, his lips warm against her cold ones. Then he was gone, running after Mitch, and she was left standing with her fingers pressed against the place where his lips had been, trying to believe she could hope.

Quinn hurried after Mitch, holding a picture of Ellie in his mind—wet and bedraggled, wearing rubber boots and a too-big poncho, dark hair plastered to her face, a streak of mud on her cheek. She was beautiful. His heart cramped. Beautiful.

But this situation wasn't beautiful. He joined Mitch and a handful of others behind the fragile barrier of sandbags.

"...afraid the bridge might go if the pressure is too great," Mitch was saying.

Quinn frowned at the old iron bridge that should have been replaced long ago. "I think we've got a more immediate problem." He pointed. "Look at the debris stuck against the center piling. If that mess doesn't break free, it could turn the bridge into a dam, sending all that water surging right for us."

Mitch caught on quickly. "If it does, we'll be lucky to have anything on River Street left standing."

Quinn nodded, fear clutching his heart. Had Ellie done what he told her and moved to safer ground?

Probably not. She wasn't a person who'd seek safety when she thought she was needed here.

"Let's take a closer look." He grabbed a metal pole from the debris washed to the bank and jogged toward the bridge, hearing Mitch's footsteps splash along behind him.

The iron bridge trembled under their feet, shaking in the onslaught of water. The roar of the river was so loud, Mitch had to shout to be heard. "What do you think?"

"I think the state should have replaced this relic years ago." Quinn reached the center and leaned over the railing, scanning the expanse of brown water roiling below. The root system of a massive spruce had caught on the middle piling, with smaller debris stacking up behind it with terrifying speed.

"We've only got another foot or so between the water and the deck. It's not going to take much to turn the whole bridge into a dam." Quinn reached for the pole, and Mitch put it in his hand.

He leaned over, the metal railing hard against his stomach, poking at the mass. "No good." He straightened, shoving the hood of his poncho back. "I can't get a good enough angle. I'll have to get outside the railing to do it."

"No, you don't." Mitch grabbed his arm before

he could move. "I'm the police chief, remember? They pay me to do the dirty jobs."

"Wait. Maybe we should get more help." Quinn glanced toward the shore.

Mitch slung his leg over the metal rail. "No time for that." He flashed a grin. "Just hold on, buddy, unless you want to chase me all the way to the Chesapeake Bay. I'm counting on you."

Mitch knelt on the narrow ledge outside the railing, taking the pole in both hands. Quinn grabbed his belt and braced both feet against the metal post. No time to look toward the bank, no time to wonder if Ellie and his mother were watching. Only time enough to breathe a wordless prayer.

Then Mitch was leaning perilously over the river, poking at the mass of debris with both hands, the only thing between him and disaster the grip of Quinn's hands.

"Almost got it." Mitch grunted, shoving harder, his weight putting an almost unbearable pressure on Quinn's arms. Pain burned along the muscles, and he gritted his teeth.

I won't let him down, Lord. I've got another chance here, and I won't let him down.

A final shove, a final scream of exhaustion from his aching muscles. Then a creak, a crash and the debris washed free.

Mitch lurched, dangling over the edge for an instant. Quinn hauled him back, both of them stumbling as he came over the railing. Quinn found his balance and clutched Mitch's arm. "You okay?"

"Thanks to you." Mitch pounded his shoulder. "Let's get out of here."

They stumbled back off the bridge, to be met by a rush of people. Quinn could hear Mitch giving orders to post watchers on the bridge to prevent any further pileups, but he didn't pay attention.

There was only one voice he wanted to hear. He pushed through the crowd, scanning faces. Only one face he wanted to see.

Ellie splashed through the muddy water toward him and ran straight into his arms.

Dawn streaked the sky with pink and gold. Ellie sat on a pile of sandbags and leaned back wearily against the side of the police car. She glanced around. Everyone else seemed to be doing the same thing—too tired to move, probably. Not that there was much more they could do, except wait for the river to crest.

She looked at the man who sat next to her. Quinn stretched and rubbed reddened eyes, then passed his hand over a stubble of beard, leaving a streak of mud in its wake.

"You should go up to the house," he said again,

as he'd said several times during the night. "Mom has a room ready for you."

"I need to be here until we know it's over." *With you.* But she couldn't quite say that, not yet. Quinn had held her in his arms, he'd kissed her with a kind of hungry gratitude when he'd come off the bridge after risking his life for all of them.

But she still didn't know what his return meant for her. And she couldn't ask. It was for him to say.

Quinn wrapped his hand around hers. "At least it hasn't gone up any more in the last two hours. If there's not a problem upriver, maybe we're going to get through this one."

Maybe. She glanced toward the shop, standing inches from disaster. "And the next one? How often can we go through this?"

"Not again." His grip tightened. "Not if I can help it."

Hope began to stir, a faint flutter in her heart. "What do you mean?"

He managed a smile. "Like my mother said, there's plenty of work for an engineer in Pennsylvania. I'm going to ask for a transfer to the local corps district. It's time I came home."

"Your mother and Kristie will be so happy." A sobering thought struck her. "Of course, then you'll be close if they reschedule the parole hearing, too."

His mouth tightened as he stared out at the brown

water, and then he faced her. "No. I won't be going to any parole hearings."

Her gaze clung to his. "Are you sure?" She could barely breathe for hoping.

He nodded. "I had time to think about it, sitting out on that back road while everyone I cared about was in trouble. God had a hard lesson for me to learn about forgiveness. But I think He finally got it through my thick head." Warmth lightened his gray eyes. "Thanks to you."

Tears trembled on the edge of spilling over, and she blinked them back. "I'm glad."

"Ellie, I—"

The siren blared on the police car, making both of them jump. Quinn got up, pulling Ellie to her feet. Her heart thumped uncomfortably. Bad news?

Mitch stood on the seat of the police car, hanging on to the roof, as people turned toward him, faces apprehensive.

"News from upriver," he shouted. "They just checked the gauges again. The crest has passed— the water's going down. We've done it!"

The crowd erupted, hugging each other, shouting and cheering and crying. Ellie choked back a sob as she turned to Quinn. "We're safe. We came through it."

He held both her hands in his. "What is it Pastor

Richie always says at baptism? Through the water, into new life.''

He glanced at the people surrounding them, then drew her behind the police car, hidden from the crowd.

''New life,'' he said again. ''That's what I want, Ellie. A new life, with you.'' He touched her face gently. ''My wise little daughter always knew you were the wife God picked out for me. It just took a little longer for me to get the message. I love you, Ellie. Will you marry me?''

She looked up at him, heart full, and saw that all the bitterness had disappeared from his face. The steady light of love glowed in his eyes, so intense it took her breath away. She could only nod and lift her face for his kiss.

Epilogue

An autumn leaf drifted into Quinn's lap as he sat on a folding chair in the park two months later. They had been months filled with changes, months of hard work. The park was just beginning to look normal again, with the fences replaced, the pavilions repaired and new grass sprouting up through the layer of mud left by the flood. Funds from the belated craft fair had paid for that. And now the community had gathered to thank God that they'd come through the water, to new life.

A lump formed in his throat as he reached to his right to take Ellie's hand. Her fingers closed around his, and her engagement ring pushed into his skin, reminding him again just how fortunate he was. She smiled at him, and her face held such happiness and contentment that it seemed to shout.

Kristie leaned forward from her seat on the other side of Ellie. His daughter had been taking a proprietary air toward their engagement, apparently convinced that only her prayers had brought it about. Well, maybe she had a point there.

"Isn't it going to start soon, Daddy?" she asked in a stage whisper.

"Soon, sweetheart," he murmured, smiling at her. "Be patient."

As if he'd heard, Pastor Richie stepped to the makeshift platform. The sun slanted on the peaceful river behind him, turning its rippling surface to gold. He raised his hands.

"Let us give thanks to the Lord, for He is good. His steadfast love endures forever." A smile lit his face. "My dear friends, God truly is good, and His love does endure. In all the hours we fought the flood, one verse kept coming back to me. 'Many waters cannot quench love; rivers cannot wash it away.' We are the living proof of that."

Quinn clasped Ellie's hand tighter as he looked at the faces surrounding him. His mother, serene as she locked hands with Charles, and beyond them Brett and Rebecca. His sister's hand was curved across the maternity blouse that announced new life. Mitch and Anne Donovan were together, with their children close at hand. Alex Caine and his new bride, Paula, had their son between them. The rest of Bedford Creek filled the chairs and stood around the edges of the seats. Even young Robbie, fidgeting on his seat, turned around to smile at him.

Many waters cannot quench love; rivers cannot wash it away.

Quinn's heart seemed to overflow with gratitude for the love surrounding him. He'd spent too long running away from this place. He squeezed Ellie's hand again. He'd come home at last, to the place where he belonged, and he'd found the love that waited here for him.

* * * * *

Dear Reader,

I'm so glad you decided to pick up this book. The love story of Ellie and Quinn lets me, like Quinn, return to Bedford Creek and find out what's been happening there. I'm delighted to revisit old friends, and I hope you will be, too.

I felt the HOMETOWN HEROES miniseries wouldn't be complete unless the town faced a flood, since the flood in the past ran through all the stories. Writing about it made me relive our own experiences in the Agnes flood of 1972. Those of us who were there will not forget!

But I suppose all of us face flood times in our lives. My hope for you is that, like the characters of my story, you'll come through the water to new life.

Please let me know how you liked this story. You can reach me c/o Steeple Hill Books, 300 East 42nd St., New York, NY 10017.

Best wishes,

Marta Perry

Next Month
From Steeple Hill's

Love Inspired®

A GROOM WORTH WAITING FOR

by *Crystal Stovall*

Jilted at the altar by her fiancé, Amy Jenkins vows to start a new life in Lexington, Kentucky. But her plans go terribly awry when she's held up in a convenience store robbery! Having survived the attack thanks to a dynamic stranger, she finds herself drawn deeply into Matthew Wynn's life. Does God's plan for her future include finding in Matthew a groom worth waiting for?

Don't miss
A GROOM WORTH WAITING FOR
On sale November 2001

Love Inspired®

Next Month From Steeple Hill's

Love Inspired

LOVE ONE ANOTHER

by *Valerie Hansen*

Romance blooms when Zac Frazier and his little boy move into Tina Braddock's quaint neighborhood. Although the compassionate day-care worker knows the pitfalls of letting anyone get too close, she can't resist extending a helping hand to the dashing single dad and his adorable son. But a heavy-hearted Tina fears that their blossoming relationship will wilt if her shameful secret is ever exposed. Turning to the good Lord for support, Tina can only pray for the inner strength she desperately needs to trust in the power of love....

Don't miss
LOVE ONE ANOTHER
On sale November 2001

Love Inspired